Holme Lee

The Beatiful Miss Barrington

Vol. III

Anatiposi

Holme Lee

The Beatiful Miss Barrington

Vol. III

Reprint of the original.

1st Edition 2023 | ISBN: 978-3-38210-309-5

Anatiposi Verlag is an imprint of Outlook Verlagsgesellschaft mbH.

Verlag (Publisher): Outlook Verlag GmbH, Zeilweg 44, 60439 Frankfurt, Deutschland
Vertretungsberechtigt (Authorized to represent): E. Roepke, Zeilweg 44, 60439 Frankfurt, Deutschland
Druck (Print): Books on Demand GmbH, In de Tarpen 42, 22848 Norderstedt, Deutschland

THE
BEAUTIFUL MISS BARRINGTON.

By HOLME LEE,

AUTHOR OF "SYLVAN HOLT'S DAUGHTER," "FOR RICHER, FOR POORER," "BASIL GODFREY'S CAPRICE," ETC. ETC.

IN THREE VOLUMES.

VOL. III.

LONDON:
SMITH, ELDER & CO., 15, WATERLOO PLACE.
1871.

CONTENTS.

THE

BEAUTIFUL MISS BARRINGTON.

CHAPTER I.

WHAT THE VILLAGE THOUGHT OF IT.

Doubtless it is impertinent of little people to discuss the affairs of the great; to proclaim the secrets of the Squire's household in the market-place; but they *will* do it; vulgar ignorance and vulgar curiosity pervade all orders of men, and the doings and misdoings at Stoneleigh Manor furnished fine themes for calumny in the village during the fall of this year.

The chief handle of malevolent speculation was provided for the gossips by the frequent appearances upon the scene of Mr. Tom Bethell. He perambulated the property hither and thither, inquiring about their work of woodmen, keepers, and labourers, with the voice of a master. He was seen often in confabulation with the steward, who grew respectful to the heir; and when the busy days of harvest were over there was a mending of roads, a repairing of fences, and planting of young copses that recalled the ancient thrifty, stitch-in-time management of the old Bethells.

Parallel with these improvements out of doors ran retrenchments in. The staff of servants was ruthlessly cut down by more than one half, the most modern and expensive taking their departure. The old butler stayed—he had been in the service of Felicia's grandfather—and the second gardener, and Bob, the head groom, who dated from the same period. Carr only saved her place by consenting to turn housemaid; and one man and a boy and four women were soon all that remained of the large establishment which, whether necessary or not at the Manor, nobody had ever anticipated seeing diminished. Miss Reed, and Mr. Barrington's valet, a supple, clever Italian, were not discharged; Miss Reed was indispensable to her patron at Ringwood, and as for his Italian, Mr. Barrington vowed himself unable to live without him—but *he* had never been reckoned amongst the regular servants, on account of his prolonged absences with his master. Mr. Tom Bethell bore the surly execrations of all who suffered from the curtailed hospitalities of the Manor. Mr. Barrington looked handsome and languid, he had been ill and had got into scrapes, but that was no reason why Tom Bethell should come playing the tyrant at Stoneleigh as if it belonged to him. Some of the people took it into their heads that he meant to worm himself into possession, and whispered significantly that he was not the man to stick at his means of doing it.

Felicia and I never made these things a subject of conversation. I do not think she cared for them at all. She was passive and indifferent to whatever did not affect her father, and to him she was mechanically and untiringly devoted. He little deserved it! It was wonderful what a transformation had come over my charming and elegant kinsman. The suavity of his manner, the indolent easiness of his temper had quite disappeared under the stress of his adversity. He was petulant, harsh, and often quite unreasonable. I shame to remember it, but he made Felicia his butt. At the first shock it was unaccountable to me how he could bear to see that sad sweet face of hers quiver with pain at his ironical and sarcastic speeches. Her very loving meekness irritated him—perhaps because he recollected how much he had sinned against her. I have seen her eyes fill and her lips tremble as she smiled to please him, but I never heard her utter a retort to his unkindness. That he was bored almost to extinction by this life which he had made so empty for them both, he never tried to conceal; the monotony of it, cut off from all his choice excitements, was too much for his calm endurance, and like many another pleasant, popular man, he proved to be gentle only when all went well with him. It was most touching to watch Felicia's poor, ineffectual wiles to amuse him; the way she showed her entire dependence upon him was the most pathetic thing I ever witnessed. And oh, how cruel often were his looks and words!

I have said before that Felicia was universally beloved in the village. There was not a house where her trouble was not known and deplored. Captain Gresham had created a warm interest by the brave figure he made at the Peace celebration, and the people had agreed that he was worthy of their young lady. Her sorrows met me everywhere in their sympathetic chat, and exercised my discretion of speech severely not to admit or deny too much. They saw her driving every day with her father to take the air; and they saw her in her accustomed place at church, but elsewhere they missed her. I think she shrank from their honest but too out-spoken pity; for she ceased to frequent the cottages where she was most familiar, though the poor, the sick, and all who needed it, were still fed by her orders. Friends and neighbours called, and repeated their calls, but she returned none. Motherly Mrs. Claylands lectured her on the enervating effects of such seclusion, and the dowager besought her with clasped hands to make an effort towards fulfilling her social duties. But as the days went on, she retired more and more from the faces of men. Sir Bevis was a deerhound in the prime of life now, and he and Tib, his playfellow, were Felicia's favourite companions. Her father talked much and wearisomely; her ears must have ached for silence often, and the dogs could only look their thoughts out of beautiful soft brown eyes.

Lame Simeon *loquitor*:—"What I says is, there's folks a bonny sight wickeder than any that's hanged at the 'sizes; ay, and many a man besides Judas as betrays them that loves 'em with a kiss. Bethell now, and Barrington, —I should like to know what Barrington thinks to himself when he comes upon his poor lass, sitting on the steps, all in a maze and a dream, with them dumb beasts at her feet. Old Bob, he brought her mare round t'other day to coax her to have a ride, but she only laid her cheek against the sensible cretur's neck and cried. 'Lor,' said Bob, 'I could ha' cried too for company, only to see how she's fallen away and lost her colour.'"

My nurse was the recipient of the old gardener's sentiments, loudly enough enunciated to reach my ears in the parlour. Nurse replied that the poor young lady fretted so after the captain that it pitied one to see her; and lame Simeon rejoined that it would afford him intense satisfaction to hear of the captain coming back, and carrying off his sweetheart, in spite of cruel father and greedy uncle.

"It is devoutly to be wished, but there's no chance of it—he's gone to get himself killed in India, where there's some terrible fighting going on," says nurse.

Lame Simeon groaned audibly that he could see no sense in *that*, and bent again to his interrupted task.

On another occasion I had the benefit of widow Burt's views, and of the land-steward's, as by her reported. "Spencer do say as the whole thing lies in a nutshell:—if the young lady don't marry to have heirs, Ringwood will just step into all when she dies, and that's what he's working for underhand. Nay, I telled Spencer, it is only kings plays that wicked game—common folks know that it don't profit a man tho' he gain the whole world, if he lose his own soul. And I should call it a sin worthy the damnation of hell to hinder that sweet lady of her mate—the beauty she was on Peace Day—you'll remember, ma'am? my poor Lucy never tired of praising her; and the captain was a sightly gentleman, as tall an' straight he was, as my Tom. And he's gone to India, Spencer says; and I suppose it's true from the way the lady looks? She's only been over my door-stone once since she came home; but I'm to carry the bairn up to the Manor twice a week. Bless her for a dear, kind lady! The Lord give her her heart's desire, or grace to forbear it!"

It is probable that the land-steward's words travelled further than he intended; for he got his discharge shortly, and Mr. Tom Bethell undertook to save his niece the expense of such a functionary, in future, by doing his duties himself, with the assistance of an ordinary labourer who had been employed by Spencer, a man of considerable natural shrewdness, but ignorant as most of his class—unable, indeed, to read or write decently. Spencer revenged his dismissal by publishing his opinions of Ringwood in all companies where he might be, until a letter from a lawyer, threatening him with an action for libel, drove him to make a public apology in the Gladestone papers. But he still continued to back his judgment amongst safe and discreet people, and that the opinion of the most sagacious went with him was proved by his prompt engagement under Mr. Falkner. Mr. Tom Bethell, in fact, fell into very evil odour at this period; into much worse odour than Mr. Barrington, who had made him his opportunities. But so it is—the blame of this world is very seldom justly apportioned.

The deposition of Spencer and the promotion of Judd, his underling, was generally regarded by the tenants as a penny-wise and pound-foolish measure. Spencer had been an excellent steward; he knew his business thoroughly, would do his best by the property as far as he was allowed, and not wrong his employers of a penny. He had narrow notions of the rights of the poor, and he and his young mistress had come to words more than once about his over-rigid interpretation of her privileges; but she entertained, notwithstanding, a sincere liking and respect for the man who, since her girlhood, had encouraged her interest in the estate, and had been proud to walk over it with her, and instruct her in that common knowledge which he was used to say it behoved a landed lady to possess. He had succeeded the unfortunate Benson, with increased responsibilities, and higher wages, and when the day arrived which was to terminate his trust and service, he insisted upon formally resigning his keys of office and his books to his mistress. And on this occasion he spoke a warning which has been quoted in these later times as over-true, though it was left unheeded while it might have been of use.

"There's Judd, Miss, that Mr. Bethell has taken such a fancy to—if he don't mind, Judd will be too many for his master; he is one of those cunning, crafty, clever chaps that are honest with good looking after, and not else. He'll soon find out that Mr. Bethell is a soft about timber, and lots of things, and he'll take advantage if he sees a fair chance, till what Mr. Bethell reckons a saving in my wages will be lost ten times over in small cheatery. This is a word to the wise, Miss, and you can pass it on."

Felicia did pass it on; but Mr. Tom Bethell, with all his covetous aspirations after the property, and all his ardent desire to restore it to its ancient value, was too fast set in his confirmed indolent habits, to be an efficient check upon a sharp practitioner like Judd; and Spencer had been a very little while gone from Stoneleigh, before it became a common saying amongst the people, that "*That* gentleman was feathering his nest warmly." And when winter arrived, complaints were rife amongst the poorer sort of the hard measure he dealt them in windfalls of wood, which had been heretofore their perquisite. We heard everything at the Rectory, but Felicia was told little or nothing now of what occurred in the village, and many abuses crept in which it would have grievously mortified her to be made acquainted with.

All through this autumn was going on the canvass for a county election. The late member had died towards the end of the session, and a hard fight was promised for the honour of succeeding him. The Marquis of Leigh had issued an address on the Liberal side, and Mr. Pollexfen, of Marsh-holms, came forward as a candidate of the most staunch Conservative principles. It was almost certain that Mr. Pollexfen would be the one to win; for he was a wealthy man, of old standing in Gladeshire, and of unimpeachable character. What the Marquis was all the world knew, and outside the pound of the family influence, only those amiable, credulous persons who believed that the House of Commons would prove a Reformatory School for the noble reprobate, were likely to give him their voices. Many gentlemen, Arthur, Squire Sylvester, and Squire Claylands, for instance, declared that they should not vote at all; they would not send a Tory to

Parliament, and they would not have a rake of quality for their representative. The deceased member was one of the old Whigs, and that the Marquis should propose to fill his place was enough to make him rise from his grave. No such alarming apparition was, however, necessary to scare the community into the exercise of their proper wits. A fresh element had been lately infused into the county society which was soon found to have leavened the whole mass. Mr. Falkner coolly asked at a director's meeting: Why not propose a second Liberal candidate, and let him try it out at the poll with the Marquis and the Tory? Another man of business said: Would Mr. Falkner stand himself? there was no man more likely to carry the suffrages of the majority, in *his* opinion. Mr. Falkner said, he did not care about going into Parliament at present, but if a requisition was made him with a fair number of signatures, he *would* stand—always supposing that they did not light on a better man.

To oppose the Castle was a dreadful, an

appalling manifestation to the feudal notions of a few; but the result proved that voters, nowadays, do not live in bodily fear of great lords; for when the day of election came, and the poll was taken, Mr. Falkner headed it, and the Marquis was more than three hundred votes behind Mr. Pollexfen. The defeat of his son was said to have disappointed the Duke exceedingly, and Lady Augusta, to signalize her displeasure at the offence which had been committed against the ducal dignity, persuaded her father that he was not well, and bade the doctors order him to spend the winter in a warmer climate. The Duke allowed himself to be convinced of the non-existent necessity, the Castle closed its gates for the season, and the great folks migrated to Mentone only to return with the swallows.

We should have endured their absence at Stoneleigh with perfect philosophy had it not led to a change there also. Lady Augusta assured Mr. Barrington that the one thing needful to complete his cure was a residence in the same beautiful Italian town as was to be honoured by her own residence. She was afraid that it would be very dull, but they must be society for each other, and Mr. Barrington knew how much her father, the Duke, liked him personally. The suggestion was only too welcome to the convalescent, heartily tired of the domestic repose of home. He mentioned it to Felicia as quite a good plan, and evidently expected her instant consent to it. There was no question of her going with him; but then, as he said, she would have Miss Reed.

Felicia heard his proposal with acute dismay, and asked why she should not accompany him? He did not absolutely say *No*, but he demurred—would evidently prefer to be free to go alone; and said they would talk about it another day. Meanwhile, Felicia spoke to me.

"I have a positive dread of being left here without any spur to compel me to rouse myself, and I have no spirits to entertain my girl-friends; besides, Rosy and Blanche don't care to come except the Manor is gay," she said. "While papa is with me I have enough to do to entertain him, which drags me out of my misery. I don't want to give way, or to break down. I wish he would take me to Mentone; I enjoyed that journey he took me to Italy after mamma died. The sight of strange places and strange people would do me good; I have a craving for change of scene like the craving of a thirsty person for a draught of pure water. If papa would only let me go to Mentone with him, I feel as if in the spring I might come to life again—it is very hard to die outright, Cousin Clare, when one is young."

My advice to her was to insist upon going; not to consult the whims of her father so much, but to assert her own reasonable desires—to exercise, in fact, a judicious selfishness. She endeavoured to do so, but not to any purpose. Mr. Barrington had an exquisite plausibility. He showed that if Felicia went, Janet must also go; and how, instead of the inexpensive system of living *en pension* which he should prefer for himself, they would have to hire a house and foreign servants, and to spend four times as much money as would suffice to set him on his balance again. The dowager and Mr. Tom Bethell gave their voices against the needless extravagance of Felicia and her maid wintering abroad; and thought, besides, that Felicia was, for the present, decidedly better at home with her friends (it appeared that they did not count her *father* amongst them). They did not disguise their opinion that Mr. Barrington might have re-established his health quite as effectually at the Manor as at Mentone, but it was less easy to thwart his will than to set aside his daughter's. He pledged himself to the avoidance of play and the observance of economy; and as his temptations were not likely to be great in the society of the Duke and Lady Augusta, when he left Stoneleigh in November, with his Italian valet, Mr. Tom Bethell did not grumble so seriously as might have been expected. I should have said that he was rather cheerful, on the contrary, and he promised Felicia to take excellent care of her in her father's absence.

I imagine that the last days of Mr. Barrington

and his daughter at home together were not happy. He betrayed great satisfaction at his escape from the monotony of Stoneleigh, and talked much of the sunny pleasures to which he looked forward. He was in more haste to depart than he need have been, for the weather was still open when he left. His good-bye seemed to turn Felicia to stone—it was negligent, unloving, indifferent, even contemptuous of her regret. He professed not to have much faith in the sincerity of her affection for himself, because she could not perfectly dissimulate every feeling besides; and his parting words were to that effect, coupled with a warning to be merrier when he came back, lest he should be scared into running away from her again. I heard him say this, while Felicia stood drooping and quivering from head to foot. When he was gone, I carried her home with me.

"It is of no use caring for anything," she replied to my exhortation to make the best of it and not to care. "It seems that only now am I beginning to realize what I have done. You spoke like an oracle, Cousin Clare—Papa accepted the sacrifice of my love, and thus he makes light of it—so you foretold that he would do. I am justly punished—justly punished, unhappy that I am!"

She was dry-eyed now, and this mood pained me even more than her days of tears. There was a profounder hopelessness in her sorrow.

Mr. Barrington's departure set the village talking anew. Felicia's filial piety was vastly admired amongst the simple folk, who said she deserved a kinder father. "The least he could have done after sending her sweetheart to the world's end, was to stay by her himself. Gone to get well? He's well enough as he is, and a deal better than some folks mind seeing him!" This was a very strong opinion, only said aside, but said with unction amongst a few, who believed that if Mr. Barrington were out of the way, and the young lady *real* mistress at the Manor, all the good customs of the old family would come back again.

Alas! we have not seen them yet!

CHAPTER II.

ONE CHRISTMAS EVE.

FROM the day that her father left her, Felicia's melancholy visibly increased. It was a dismal season. Snow fell early in December, but only enough to spoil the green country without clothing it in the white splendour of Christmas raiment. On the sparse snow followed a bitter black frost which bound the roads and streams like iron.

I remember going to the Manor on one of the dreariest of these afternoons. The door was opened by Carr, who said the old butler was ill of asthma, and had fallen asleep by the kitchen fire. The picture-gallery felt as cold as a church on a week-day, and pointing to the empty stoves, Carr remarked that her hands were full enough of work in that great house, without kindling fires that nobody saw. The library was the warmest, cosiest room in this weather, and there lived Miss Reed—Miss Felicy lived upstairs in her mamma's room, and only came down to the library for dinner and lunch, and not always for those meals.

A few words here of the duenna. Miss Reed had kept herself in the back-ground, and had exercised infinite discretion during the passage of recent events. She was growing fat, and wore a countenance of serene feline content. If Felicia did not give her much of her society, she never hurt her feelings by rude speeches, or interfered with her placid self-indulgence. The duenna was in comfortable quarters, warm, well-fed and lazy; and when she was very dull, there was either the remembrance or the anticipation of a visit from Mr. Tom Bethell, who called to see her continually, but did not often see Felicia. She excused herself nine times in ten, Miss Reed informed me; adding, of her own opinion, that the poor young lady was very peculiar, and she could not make her out at all—whether it was temper ailed her, or grief, or the incubation of some serious illness that would prostrate her by and by. These things distressed me to see and hear exceedingly; but there was no present remedy, and I neither feared nor suspected more than I was actual witness of.

That afternoon I found Felicia—as she was usually to be found at this time of day—seated at a table between the fire and the oval window, her pen-and-pencil diary open before her, and the dainty, elegant means of adding to its records carefully set out by Janet. She had written nothing in the beautiful volume since she was last at Hampton Court, but she had touched in three landscape bits, from memory or from fancy, I know not which:—a sunrise on a far-stretching plain, very sweet, hushed and solitary; a robin at a cottage window, and a river-bank with tall flags and moonlight reflections in the water—all scenes of peace and home-quiet. Her imaginations were never gloomy, austere or terrible.

She changed her seat to the couch when I went in, and began to say that she had received only one letter from Mentone, though her father had been gone nearly a month. "Sometimes I think the postman must be dead, I have so few letters now." I suggested as the probable cause, that she did not answer those she received. She confessed that she did not, and added, "I have nothing to write about. Oh! you don't know how I miss Paul's dear letters!" And her lover having been mentioned, she talked of him on and on, as she invariably did when we were alone, reciting incidents that I knew by heart—I will not say, until my ears were weary of the bootless tale—but till the afternoon was gone. And this description of one visit will suffice for a description of many at this period.

It was a relief to her thus to talk, but it made me more and more anxious. I engaged Arthur to counsel her against the growing evil of letting one miserable idea tyrannize over her senses to the exclusion of every other interest. I was very sad to see how she, who was formerly such a religious creature, forsook her good works, her Bible, and even her prayers. One day she saw my eye rest on the shelf where lay her books of piety—her mamma's books—dusty as they never used to be when she was happy and enjoyed her morning and evening readings; and as I looked from them to her, deprecating such neglect, she understood me and laughed—I cannot tell how that laugh shocked me, its cynical ring was so unlike her natural mirth.

I feared to say too much on this painful, perilous phase of sentiment, so I said nothing—she knew, indeed, all that I could have said; and Arthur dealt more authoritatively with her sick soul than I should have dared to do. But he did not find her easy to convince. She was evidently setting her heart in resentment against her sorrow and against heaven.

Mr. Cartwright and my sister Helen were now home again at Beechcroft, and I invited Felicia more than once to drive over with me and see them. But she had always an excuse, and when Helen came to the Rectory, and called upon her, she was not admitted. There had ever been reserve in their friendship, and Felicia pleaded, in extenuation of her rudeness, that time, and what had happened since their parting, had made them almost strangers. I argued against this nonsense; but her taste for seclusion had now come to such a pass that she would see no one if she could avoid it—*no one*—not even her grandmamma. I believe she would have shut me out, but I was patient with her long plaints and memories of her lover.

We hear constantly of girls in similar case betaking themselves to much church-going, to fasting, to visiting and nursing the poor—a very salutary refuge and defence against pernicious idleness; but Felicia did not discipline her spirit after this sort. She fasted and practised certain austerities, but all in solitude. Janet told me that she ate scarcely enough to keep life in a bird; she refused meat and wine; and, said the servant, "When she sleeps it is on the bare boards. I found her one morning lying along the floor, and her dear face was so peaceful I had not the heart to wake her; when I said after how foolish it was, with a good bed to lie on, she answered that she was following the dictates of nature and conscience in lying and living hard, and it was a penance for her sins. She says very queer things sometimes, poor young lady; I should not like everybody to hear them."

I kept to myself what Janet told me, not, in fact, seeing much in it. Sleeping on the bare boards was much better than not sleeping at all: to cease from wine and dainty meats and soft cushions was not likely to injure a fine, strong constitution like Felicia's, and if the denial was a solace to her wounded mind, as probably it was, she did well to persevere in it. But it could not fail that unpleasant rumours should creep out and spread, and exaggerated fears be suggested by the ignorant.

When these fears and rumours were reported to me, I treated them with disdain; but a few days before Christmas certain incidents occurred, which excited my suspicion, and put me on my guard. There is a danger in letting lies go uncontradicted and undisproved, when the disproof of them is easy; the popular idea then becomes that what is not denied must be true. I hold that neither man nor woman is bound to answer an anonymous, false accusation, though it may have spread world-wide, and be almost as widely credited; but there are instances in which my theory must yield to custom, and let the defence speak, and Felicia's was an instance in point.

One morning I overtook Mr. Tom Bethell in the village; he had just been to wish Felicia and Miss Reed the compliments of the coming season, he said, but he had only seen Miss Reed. As we were walking in the same direction, we walked on together, and my companion began to ask me what I thought of Felicia, adding that he was afraid my influence was not so powerful with her as it had once been. I let the inuendo pass, and said what I thought—that give her time and she would recover her tone—youth and health were all in her favour.

Mr. Tom Bethell shook his head negatively: "She is falling into a very bad way. Miss Reed's account of her is truly alarming. I have thought proper to write to her father about it."

"I see her every day, and am not alarmed. If she were ill, Janet would know it—Janet is wise and watchful as a mother for her. You know as well as I do that if a doctor, a man of sense, saw her, he would advise to give her back her lover. Captain Gresham could do her more good than the whole college of physicians."

"That is a prescription that we cannot afford, dear Mrs. Gower," was the answer I got. "Captain Gresham is in India, and signalizing himself there as highly as he did in the Crimea, I am told. Felicia has made her moan for him too long, considering how readily he gave her up—much more readily than we expected."

"I perceived no readiness in his giving-up. You know best what terror for her father was made to act upon Felicia's mind."

"Her *mind*, poor girl, *that* is what we tremble for—her mind giving way," said her uncle dolefully.

I was silent for a minute; but catching a glimpse of a certain eagerness in his eyes, set on my face, I said with some scorn, "You need neither fear it nor *hope* it. Felicia's mind is as firm as a rock."

He smiled with disagreeable significance; said the maladies of a love-sick girl were rarely irretrievable, and then, being come to a path through the fields by which he was going to meet Judd, we wished each other a good morning, and parted with anything but a friendly feeling in our hearts.

Preparations for Christmas were now in progress at the Manor. The bounties were to be distributed on Christmas Eve in the servants' hall, as the old custom was, and I had promised Felicia to select the gifts, to apportion them according to the needs of the poor, and to make the distribution, if she felt unequal to the effort when the day came. Miss Reed had offered to take the work on herself, but Felicia had said rather curtly: "No, Mrs. Gower is the proper person, the rector's wife, if I cannot act for myself."

"But you *will* act for yourself, dear, and Miss Reed and I will help you," I had added quickly, for the duenna blinked angrily at us both, and I was all for peace with her—I hardly know why—

perhaps because I was secretly afraid of her, much as I am afraid of the black adder in our woods, which I would not tread on for all I am worth.

On the day when I had the foregoing conversation with Mr. Tom Bethell, word was sent me that the blankets, flannel, and warm clothing that had been ordered from Gladestone, had arrived, and awaited my inspection; and immediately after lunch, I went across to the Manor, to see to the unpacking, and to divide them into portions, as they were to be given away. The task would be long and heavy, and I thought to myself that I would invite Miss Reed's assistance, to please her, if possible. I was so regularly at the Manor this winter, that my coming and going was a matter of course. Carr admitted me, and I used to find my way to the boudoir, where I was daily expected in the gloaming. I did not often break in on Miss Reed's privacy, but on this occasion I asked Carr to announce me to her in the library, which she did—as I remembered later, after knocking at the door, and receiving permission to come in. It was impossible not to notice that my appearance was a surprise, and a most unwelcome surprise; it even caused me to halt a few paces from the door, and to say, with an amused smile, that if I disturbed her, I would instantly run away.

But she disclaimed anything pressing in her occupation, and was urgent that I should draw near the fire and take a chair; which I did rather reluctantly, for she was busy writing, and shuffled a large folio sheet, covered with her scratchy caligraphy, under some clean sheets, as if I might spy its contents, were it exposed to view. The table was littered with books, old and new, some of which, from the air and smell of them, had long abode on their shelves undisturbed. I asked her in what abstruse study she was engaged, and opened one of the biggest and blackest tomes: *The Anatomie of Melancholie* it was called, and its yellow pages were stuffed with Latin. I clapt it up, and out flew a cloud of dust, but my mind was full of blankets and flannel, and I was beginning to speak of my business when the extraordinary suffusion and nervousness of

Miss Reed's countenance arrested and fixed my attention. I cast my eyes deliberately over the books then, and saw that all within their range treated of medical science in one form or another: *The Senses and the Intellect; The Mind in Health and Disease; Insanity; its Causes, Prevention, and Cure; The Diary of a Late Physician*, and other such kindred works.

"Well, what do you make of them?" inquired the duenna, in a voice the agitation of which she could not control; and she began to pile them up, to make her table tidy, as she said; in the course of which operation, she contrived to put the document that I had found her labouring on into the table-drawer, which she then locked. I was certainly not contemplating a raid upon her literature, but her manner was so furtive and suspicious that I did not answer her; my thoughts were lost in speculation; and probably more disquieted by my musing silence than she would have been by any question or remark, she rushed into explanation, of which I believed just so much as I knew, and no more.

"I have a poor young relative mentally afflicted, and I was looking into some of these learned books to find out what hope there is for her—I am afraid none, I am afraid *none!* It is a most fascinating study, that of insanity, if you give your mind to it, Mrs. Gower."

"It is the last study in the world that I should give my mind to," said I. "Would not you be wiser to let it alone?"

"I have been content all these years with the knowledge that we are fearfully and wonderfully made; but lately, since the affliction of that young relative whom I mentioned, a certain interest has grown up round these painful subjects."

Miss Reed was not born to be a great criminal. She quaked visibly, watched me with blinking eyes and burning cheeks. Of course, I was as well aware, as if she had said so, that the "young relative" was poor Felicia, and that the duenna and Mr. Tom Bethell were laying their heads together to see how much further for their own advantage, they could mar that blighted life.

For a minute I hesitated whether to avow my knowledge or to hide it, and pretend to be deceived. But in the first place I am unskilful at pretending, and in the next, I consider that open tactics in these cases are more likely of success than any amount of diplomacy. So I looked steadily at my adversary, and said: "Mr. Tom Bethell will be interested in your studies, for he too has a young relative for whose mind he trembles—so he informed me this morning — perhaps you are studying in company?"

Ah! the cunning little cat, she was far cleverer than I! In a moment she had the tables turned upon me! She rubbed her face to cool it, and said, with a light sigh of intense relief: "If Mr. Bethell has told you that he trembles for Miss Barrington my prudent fiction may be dropt—it is a deliverance to be quit of the need for a false pretext. But I am sorry that he should have spoken to you—I have kept my counsel from the dowager even, for she is heart-broken at the poor girl's miserable condition. It is injurious to families to have these things known; they ought to be held secret—though they very rarely are—Mr. Bethell should have remembered that he has children of his own, and that a censorious world is ever ready to attribute the calamity of an individual to hereditary defect. But you, dear Mrs. Gower, will not be of those who chatter——"

"Certainly not!" cried I, ablaze with hot indignation. "And wherever I come upon the trail of your insidious and malignant slander, you may rely upon me for stamping it out!"

"Those are strong words, Mrs. Gower," faltered the duenna.

"Not so strong as my feeling! But I thank you for having shown me where a new danger awaits my darling. You would try to make her out *mad!* Oh! but you are a wicked little woman!" With this gasp of inexpressible fury and disgust, I fled from the library to the blankets and flannel.

Arthur looked very grave when I narrated to him my discoveries of this day (he even forgot to rebuke me for losing my temper), and said that this peril was serious, indeed. He thought over it a long while, had one of his good talks with Felicia herself, and encouraged me by every means to withdraw her from her seclusion, which was sure to favour and promote the mystery that was the very atmosphere for lies to work in. At first, and while away from her, I thought that a direct warning of what threatened might be the shortest cure for her melancholy; but when I saw her next, and looked into her plaintive eyes, I could not, for my life, have breathed a word of it! Her mind was as clear and sensitive as mine was, and I had only to think a moment of how such a warning would suit myself, to know that it would be a mortal stab, too cruel for her to endure. So I held my peace, and when Janet mentioned to me significant little words and deeds that came under her observation, we agreed together that, while opposing their progress strenuously, we must, if possible, keep them from the knowledge of their helpless victim.

And now came on Christmas Eve, a public day

at the Manor formerly, but this year there were no festivities beyond the distribution of the annual gifts—yule-logs, beef, and warm clothing; and spiced-ale for a health to all comers.

The servants' hall, a large stone hall, with a gallery over the great doors, and a high Tudor window, was handsomely decorated with holly and yew, laurel and bay, and a prodigious fire of pine and oak logs on the hearth made it a genial picture of the time of year. There were generally a few friends invited, with leave to bring any stranger-guests who might be spending the Christmas-tide at their houses, for the custom was ancient in all its forms and surroundings, and was interesting for such persons to see. But no invitations at all had been sent out this year—not even to the Dower House or to Ringwood. I ventured on a remonstrance, but Felicia said: "No, I will have no merry-making under my roof. There has been a dreadful death in the house, and I am in mourning." This was one of her metaphorical speeches, which Janet called *queer*, and said she would not like them to be heard by everybody. I consented that, perhaps, her decision was wise; for who should dance when the mistress is weeping?

The cottagers trooped in at two o'clock, frosty-faced and cordial, and when they were all assembled, Janet announced the fact in the boudoir, where Felicia and I were waiting together. Janet had arrayed her young lady for the occasion beautifully—in a dress of purple silk and velvet, and with an ermine tippet on her shoulders. We were sitting close by the fire when the summons came; the blaze had caught Felicia's face, and given her a transient blush. She had not looked so lovely for many a day, and I was congratulating myself on the charming natural effect she would produce upon the people, when she annoyed and disappointed me beyond measure by saying that she would rather not go down into the hall,—she would watch the scene from the gallery. I told her she was a lazy, idle girl, and left her wistfully deprecating the reproach: "Yes, you are—a lazy, idle girl, and I shall not unsay it," I reiterated, as I shut the door upon her, vext to see how obstinately and ignorantly she was playing into the hands of her enemies.

When I reached the servants' hall, Miss Reed was already there, fussed and shaking—with *cold*, she said, but there was not cold enough to palsy the feeblest body; and a better reason for her agitation was up in the gallery, where Mr. Tom Bethell and Rosy had ensconced themselves, in company with a couple of gentlemen of pleasant aspect, perfect strangers to me. I whispered to Janet to go and warn her mistress by whom the gallery was occupied; and while I was uncomfortably reflecting how she might take this intrusion of guests uninvited, the two leaves of the great door were thrown wide open, and the old butler announced in his voice of ceremony—"The Lady of the Manor."

Young and old all stood up as Felicia walked in, very stately, very gently, the fire flush on her face still, and a little flush of pride and anger to deepen it. Behind her followed my worthy Arthur, and Sir Bevis and Tib; and as she advanced up the middle of the hall, the treble voices of the children of the choir, ranged on either side, rose in a cheerful shrill old carol, celebrating the Holy Nativity and the graces of the dwellers in that house. Felicia stood, too, till the song was done, and then seated herself in the chair of ancient state, raised three steps above the floor, where she could be seen, admired, and reverenced by all her faithful, humble friends, for whom this was the most memorable day in the year. A sense of joy and triumph rushed over me. Everything was happening according to rule and precedent; all I wished for was more witnesses.

While each of the cottagers was receiving his or her gift from the hands of the lady herself, who forgot the name of none, who inquired for absent sons and daughters, bed-ridden parents and sick children, as if she had no thought but the care of her people, the perfume of spiced ale was penetrating the chinks of the door where it was to enter by and by; and when the distribution was accomplished, mighty flagons were brought in, with cups and beakers, one of silver-gilt, jewelled and very antique, from which generations of the lords and ladies of Stoneleigh Manor had pledged their guests on Christmas Eve. Felicia rose, and with a most sweet dignity, drank to the people, who drank to her again with many happy Christmases and a hearty good cheer.

She retired from the hall, and her canine servitors in her wake, while the cheer was ringing in the high timbered roof; and as she passed Widow Burt with her grandson crowing in her arms, she stopt an instant, pressed with her finger the dimple in his cheek, and said what a bonny boy he grew. Following her out, I heard some whispered remarks of the women. "Bless her dear heart, but she *looks* nicely—she remembered my John, a pleeceman at Manchester." "Lost her wits, indeed! She's got her wits about her as much as any of us!" "The Lord be good to her, for she's good to his poor, deny it who dare!" I rejoiced in these frank personalities; if any of the people had come full of compassionate curiosity for what they might see, they would go away satisfied that, as usual, gossip told more lies than truth, even amongst good neighbours.

At the foot of the stairs Felicia turned round to me, and said: "Well, Cousin Clare, have I pleased you to-day?"

"Yes, my darling, that you have! You see it only requires a little resolution."

I was still speaking when the voices of Mr. Tom Bethell and his friends were heard in the gallery on the way to come down. We retreated into the library, but neither were we safe there. The next minute Mr. Tom Bethell entered, with a fulsome greeting and congratulation to his dear niece on her courageous effort at the performance of her Christmas-eve duties. Rosy, Miss Reed, and the two strangers had followed him in, and he now begged to introduce the strangers to Felicia as gentlemen known to her father, men of antiquarian tastes, who coming casually into the neighbourhood, had desired to see the famous Manor House of Stoneleigh. He omitted to name them, and Felicia evinced some surprise in the courtesy with which she made them welcome.

It was a most impertinent intrusion, and that the gentlemen knew it was being felt so, their countenances betrayed. They could have seen the Manor House from vault to roof-tree without seeing its mistress:—this was the vext thought that traversed my mind, as I seated myself a little apart, and watched and listened in unbounded astonishment while they made archeological and then general conversation with Felicia. Miss Reed joined in it, suggesting here a fact and there a fancy to my poor bewildered darling, in a manner the offensiveness of which I cannot describe—it was patronizing, caressing, canting, odious; and Felicia seemed equally at a loss to understand or to check it.

Rosy sat dumb as I did, but her face expressed a scared sort of pity, that perplexed me, while her father anxiously attended to every word that dropt from the lips of each speaker in turn. Into the midst of this scene, which no effort at being natural could make otherwise than awkward, entered Arthur, to announce that he had made an end of the yule-logs and roast beef, and everybody had gone home happy and contented. He was chafing his cold hands, for the logs had been distributed in the wood-house, and Felicia in her simple kind fashion invited him to take the other end of the couch next the fire, where she sat herself. Thereupon the two strangers rose, without waiting for Mr. Tom Bethell to take the initiative, and so they would have gone away, their names still a secret to us, had not Arthur, after a moment's studying gaze at the elder of the two, exclaimed: "Surely it is Dick Tuke?" and a cordial handshake ensued, signalizing the renewal of a warm school-day friendship. They had never met since they were boys together at Rugby, and Arthur seemed uncommonly glad that they had met now.

"I think, Uncle Tom, you forgot to mention the names of these gentlemen," said Felicia, and there was a thrill in her voice that drew all eyes upon her—a thrill of alarm and distress.

"Dr. Tuke and Dr. Gooch," replied her uncle, with a visage of dark confusion.

These two names in conjunction revealed a plot.

They were the names of two learned doctors, consulted in almost all the great law-suits involving questions of sanity. I hoped that they might be unfamiliar to Felicia, but in this I was mistaken; she recognised both, and put her own construction on their visit. I was amazed at the control she exercised over face and feeling as she asked, putting aside their archeological pretences, whether they had come to see her by the request of her father or by the request of Mr. Bethell. There was a momentary hesitation who should answer her, excusable under the sudden query, and she exclaimed in a most earnest, pathetic voice: "I am not mad, gentlemen, but I am a most unhappy young creature, whose enemies are stronger than her friends!"

"That is one of her fixed delusions—that we are her enemies, and hate her!" interjected Miss Reed plaintively.

Dr. Gooch smiled like a man of humour, and Felicia having risen in her energy, he took her hand reassuringly, and said: "I can certify that you are not mad—not more mad, that is, than ninety-nine in a hundred of your fellow-creatures. Most of us have a screw loose—not even excepting *you*, madame," with a side-long bow to Miss Reed, who was gaspingly impatient to explain that all had been meant for the best—she had heard that slight alienation of mind, taken in time, was easily cured, but neglected, grew as easily into confirmed insanity.

"I know where you got up your brief. It is clever, but there is no case, madam," said Arthur's friend, who spoke much less genially than Dr. Gooch. Then, addressing Felicia, he said they had her father's authority for being there, and asked to be allowed to see her in the presence of those only whom she considered her friends. There was no attempt on the part of anyone to defeat the purpose for which the doctors had come, nor on theirs any further attempt to dissimulate it.

Moved by conscience Mr. Tom Bethell, Rosy, and Miss Reed spontaneously quitted the library. Felicia looked wistfully after Rosy, but she did not bid her stay. Her strength and power of control had been severely tried to-day in more ways than one, and it was with trembling lips and tearful eyes that she professed herself ready and willing to reply to any question that the physicians might judge it expedient to ask. Dr. Gooch, in his kind paternal manner, said that they were satisfied she was perfect mistress of herself, and her father's fears had been aroused for no cause. She thanked them, and then spoke of herself more openly than I should have expected her to speak; but the physicians had either been told the truth of her story or they had divined it, and Dr. Tuke, in whom there was more appearance of severity than in his colleague, administered to her some sound counsel.

"My dear young lady, if it were your lot to work hard for your living you would recover quickly of your hurt. Without the spur of necessity there is more effort needed to keep going. You have plucked up a brave spirit to-day, which proves what you are capable of. Walk, ride, see your friends, don't forget your prayers, and in six months' time there will be no more cause to inquire into the state of your mind than there is to inquire into mine. *Mope*, and I will not answer for it but that you may become a burden to yourself, and an incurable grief to all who love you."

Felicia was gazing up at the speaker with large, frightened eyes. "Tell them to take away Miss Reed—I am afraid of her, and afraid of myself with her," said she eagerly.

"Who is Miss Reed? Oh, the lady who got up the brief. Yes, we will recommend her removal as a dangerous irritant, if you will promise to follow the sage advice of this other lady" (indicating me) "whom you appear to confide in."

"She is the only woman-friend I have since my mamma died, except mamma's maid and my nurse," replied Felicia; and then with the humility and simplicity of a child, while the tears ran down her cheeks, she gave the promise Dr. Tuke required.

It was a most sad scene, most touching and painful.

"She used not to be so weak, but *really* she is not well," said I, excusing her; for now she fairly broke out weeping.

Doctors are confessors; they know everthing, and are not often hard on poor humanity. Dr. Gooch was cheerful and soothing, but he was pitiful as well, and Felicia was sensible, even in the midst of her distress, that he was a man to make a friend of. "I have dreaded lest this should come upon me," she said, meaning this cruel imputation of insanity. "If I get worse I will send for you—I have a confidence that you will not let them use me roughly."

Here Dr. Tuke infused another dose of his tonic-bitters. "Don't let us fall on sentiment and foolish imaginations. You have good common sense, and need not lose your wits for anybody's assertion that they are gone. You are in God's hands and your own; and if you are well-advised, you will forthwith begin to do your best to resume those former habits and occupations, in which no doubt you delighted. And so you will disarm and defeat hatred, malice, and evil tongues."

"Where is the lady with the ferret-eyes gone?" Dr. Gooch inquired. "She is the worthy friend of Mr. Bethell, and my prescription is that she go and spend Christmas at Ringwood, and do not return for the New Year."

He spoke drolly, but he meant what he said, and moreover, supported by Dr. Tuke, he had it carried out. The two physicians held Mr. Barrington's permission to do and to order at their discretion whatever they judged best for his daughter—even to her removal from the Manor; and to remove from the charge of her a positively obnoxious person, who was, besides, so dull or liable to panic as to mistake sorrow for incipient madness, was a measure of the first necessity, and they insisted upon it.

Felicia retreated to her own room, and by way of softening the announcement to the duenna, Rosy was bidden to put it in the form of an invitation. But Miss Reed's shrewdness instantly discerned the truth, and she was horribly dismayed by this unexpected and precipitate conclusion to her manœuvres.

Go to Ringwood? Leave the Manor *not* to return. Was that a reward for her fidelity? Let no one expect gratitude for long service in this world! She would not go! She would stand upon her rights! If she was to be turned out of house and home without a day's warning, after twenty years in the family, let her know why. Give her a quarter's salary and her maintenance for a quarter, or——"

Mr. Tom Bethell, more humiliated and aggrieved than his wretched tool, abridged her eloquence, and in the cold winter dusk drove his party to Gladestone, where the physicians took the train for London; and then, with the addition of the duenna to his Christmas houseful, which he knew would be most unwelcome to his wife, the defeated plotter took the longest way round to Ringwood.

"Poor papa, he was afraid to face mamma, who cannot endure Miss Reed—and she *is* a disagreeable old thing," was Rosy's amiable version of the affair, to whom Miss Reed, when not of use, was as little welcome as to her step-mamma.

We had a happier Christmas-Day at Stoneleigh that she was gone. Janet and Carr spent some hours of it in carefully packing up her property to send to Ringwood next morning. "The better day, the better deed," was their reflection on their task, and no doubt but they accomplished it with hearty good-will.

CHAPTER III.

"TWO SIDES TO EVERY STORY."

The Ringwood faction had sustained a signal defeat, but everybody who knows the credulity of the world, knows by what skill of words even defeats may be turned to advantage.

When I caught Miss Reed surrounded by her literature of insanity, she was engaged in drawing up that *brief*, as the doctors called it, which, put into the hands of crotchety or unscrupulous men, might have been the instrument of consigning Felicia to the most dreadful of all imprisonments. How much the duenna believed of what she wrote, God knows; perhaps she believed it all—we may give her the benefit of the doubt. Dr. Tuke delivered it to Arthur at my request, for I was curious to see it. It was clever, as he had said, and free from extravagance, but evidently to me, drawn up from books rather than from nature; for certainly my darling was guiltless of every one of the eccentricities imputed to her, saving and excepting a genuine dislike to the imputer—which was too common to be counted an eccentricity at all.

We learned that Mr. Barrington had received a copy of this dangerous document and an alarming letter from Tom Bethell at the same time. With a sagacity which seldom distinguished him, he carried both to the Lady Augusta, who frankly said that she believed neither. "But to be safe and sure, let Tuke and Gooch see her," she advised. "If there be anything really wrong, they are the men to trust for her treatment; if there be nothing to apprehend they will say so—they are above making a case where there is no case."

Mr. Barrington, acting on this counsel, wrote instantly to the two physicians, and to Ringwood, directing Mr. Tom Bethell to make arrangements for their interview with Felicia, giving as little publicity to the unhappy occasion as possible. Miss Reed's *brief* was dispatched to prepare and forewarn them, and the event passed off as I have narrated. I wish I could add that there was an end of it; but the mere fact that two doctors, known for what they were all over the kingdom, had been down to Stoneleigh to visit Miss Barrington was susceptible of being very variously misrepresented. Even the removal of Miss Reed was talked of as her *flight* from a task too severe and trying for her nerves; and though Felicia did begin to show herself again, and was seen more or less by all the people of the neighbourhood, a notion did creep abroad, and fix itself in the belief of many that her mind was affected. Mrs. Willis, Captain Gresham's sister, who had never cordially approved of his engagement to Felicia, settled herself firmly in this conviction.

Felicia had experienced a great deliverance, Arthur told her, and she was not unthankful; but the bloom of a life is not to be restored any more than the bloom of a peach roughly handled; and the reluctant, mechanical fashion in which she went about amongst friends and acquaintances as a duty now, was very different from the spontaneous pleasantness of her former intercourse with them. And I will not deny that there was an occasional absence of manner about her, and also an occasional excitability which might help to deepen the false impression that had been created by the visit of the great doctors—for as for keeping it private, that was the last thing the Ringwood people thought of doing. They published it everywhere, with their own notes and explanations. Miss Reed's action in procuring it came to be extenuated as the result of a too tender anxiety; and Mr. Tom Bethell was gravely compassionated, as being left with the chief care of his niece upon him, and exposed to all sorts of unkind and unfair suspicions, some of which could not fail to stick, let him guide his behaviour with whatsoever discretion he might.

Till the beginning of the New Year, when Felicia paid a visit to the Dower House, she was quite alone with her servants. I hoped that her

Grandmamma Bethell and Miss Lassells might return to the Manor with her, but they did not—no one, she said, cared to come any more to that house; even her Uncle Ralph had declined her last invitation, and the Ringwood girls did not wish to come unless she could promise them some gaiety. The dowager had contracted a shyness of her once favourite, mingled of fear and remorse, which made them ill at ease together. Felicia never made her grandmamma one complaint or one reproach after the act of her sacrifice was consummated; but when the old lady looked into the girl's ruined face (and it was strange how Felicia lost her beauty at this time), she must have felt pricked in her conscience that it was a great part her work.

It made one's heart bleed to see her—her supple form how wasted, her fair complexion how dulled, her eyes how slow and wan! While she kept herself close to the house, these changes had not been so sadly conspicuous; but now that we saw her going the old round of drives, rides, walks, calls, we thought sometimes that it was a stranger we were meeting. And most of all her tuneful tongue! we never heard it now, and Janet told me that she had not opened the piano, or raised her voice to sing, since her father went to Italy. It was in everybody's mouth how Miss Barrington was altered and gone off.

As the early spring broke out of frost and snow suddenly, another evil stroke of fortune—or what we counted so—fell upon her. She caught the scarlet fever, and from my children too. They had the complaint mildly, but I insisted on exiling myself from the Manor, and in denying Felicia entrance at the Rectory, until the infectious stage of convalescence was passed. We had resumed our usual visits for a week or more before she sickened, but it was said, and perhaps with truth, that she carried the disease from our house; and a most torturing reflection it was to me when she succumbed to it, and became very ill.

It happened that before she broke down, she and I had talked of her having a lady to stay with her, in the light of a friend and companion, a successor to Helen, in fact, and she had expressed a wish that one could be found, whom she might like, and her father not disapprove. She was far too much alone, and wearied of her own sad society more and more as the spring days lengthened. It was after this conversation, and in consequence of it probably, that she wrote to Dr. Gooch to inquire if he could find her such a friend as she wanted. His reply arrived on the first day when she said to Janet, "What ails me? I cannot hold up my head," and she sent it to me with a pencil request written across, that I would answer it for her at once, and in the affirmative. Dr. Gooch's letter was a proposal that a sister of Dr. Tuke, the widow of a younger brother of his own, Mrs. Leslie-Gooch should come on a visit to the Manor for a month, which might be extended if they took kindly to each other. It was a pleasant letter, and I learnt from it that this was not the beginning of their correspondence. Felicia's directions were carried out, and two days after—the very day when our country doctor pronounced that her malady was scarlet fever, and that of a severe type—Mrs. Leslie-Gooch arrived at Stoneleigh. I went to Gladestone to meet her, and tell her the state of affairs, in case she might not choose to face the risk; for with Carr and Janet to nurse her the poor patient could not be better; but she elected to go forward to her post at once, and she was a woman of such frank courage and charity that it was all the relief imaginable to me when she pronounced her decision.

The moment that Felicia's illness took wind, Mr. Tom Bethell rode over to the Rectory (he would not go near the Manor) to get the news in full. He listened to it like a very anxious kinsman, indeed, and was pleased to express high satisfaction at there being in the house with his niece a lady of such tact and experience as Mrs. Leslie-Gooch. I asked if he knew that lady.

"Oh, yes, I know her! She took care of Cholmondeloy's poor wife—you *remember?*" I did remember; if I had not remembered, or had never heard, the odious significance of his tone would have explained what ailed that unhappy lady.

It was as well to refrain myself from anger, but the implication that Felicia needed the same care-taker as Mrs. Cholmondeloy was almost too much for my patience. He made his visit short that morning, but he repeated it the next day, and the next after that, and every day while the fever was running its course; and must have lost almost as much in weight and substance as the sick girl herself from the fever of another sort that was consuming him. He was pitiable to behold for a few days when it was impossible to say from hour to hour whether Felicia would live or die; and it was not the relief of joy that gleamed from his restless eyes, when I was, at length, able to assure him that the doctors considered the most imminent danger over, though they could only hope for a lingering and, perhaps, imperfect recovery.

All this time I had not seen my darling, nor did I see her for yet some weeks to come. Janet told me it did not matter so far as Felicia was concerned, for she would not notice me—she noticed nothing—she lay voiceless, inanimate as a picture of death with open blank eyes, and helpless and docile as a little child. Janet and Carr, those two good women, were more to her now than all the world besides, and she would have missed them more had they been taken away.

Through this cruel time I was Mr. Barrington's correspondent, and if I could have believed that his impatience for my daily bulletins had no motive but fatherly affection, he would have deserved all my compassion. But I knew what he would lose besides in losing her, and even if his letters had not betrayed his ingrain selfishness, his conduct to her both before and after would justify me in saying that his hold over her fortune was what he was most alarmed for.

Except George Sylvester, all the world avoided the Manor like a pest-house, and called only at the gardener's lodge to inquire for the young lady. George went boldly to the door, poor fellow, and would have his intelligence from Mrs. Leslie-Gooch; and there was nothing in his tears to be ashamed of when he poured out his faithful sorrow to me during the crisis of Felicia's fate. "I hate to think of her dying! She never cared much for me, but I've loved her ever since I was a boy, and all through I have kept a sort of hope that I should win her—and they have just told me it is a chance she lives to see another day!" he cried, passionately, and covered his face, and sobbed again.

However, Felicia *did* live, and George's hope lived too, though he hid it carefully; and in April the great folks, whose society her father had gone to Mentone to share, returned to the Castle. We expected that Mr. Barrington would come home too, but his letters said not yet one word of that. He had begged me to see Felicia, and to tell him truly how she looked. I could only tell him that she looked like a wraith.

It was a bright afternoon in May when I was admitted into the boudoir for the first time. Felicia now sat up for some hours, and liked to sit in the sun; but she had not breathed the air yet, and her face, with a filmy white kerchief over her head and tied under her chin, was a very ghost's for mournfulness. But the philosophical way in which she smiled at me as I sat down by her was reassuring as to the clearness of her mind; she was laughing at the solemn effect she produced on me, though her pale lips parted so languidly. Well might I be solemn.

"After a long while, here you are, Clare," said she. "Blithe little woman, put off this rueful countenance and look gay! Everybody is to be gay who comes to visit me—and the doctor says I am not to be contradicted. I am about a hundred years older than I was."

"You look so," rejoined I, taking her cue. Weak as she was in body, her spirit was stronger.

"I look like a widow in this cambric coif; but they have cut off my hair. I used to have beautiful hair."

"It will soon grow again. Jack's little poll is smooth as a billiard-ball."

"It will be darker, and not so glossy, Janet says. But I don't care." She began idly turning the rings round on my fingers, and talking softly half to herself. "They call that a *guard*, and this is the wedding-ring—I suppose, I shall never have a wedding-ring. Grannie's hands are so tiny that her wedding-ring had to be made for her; she said any common ring would do for me—would do for me." A little bird hopped on the window-sill. "See if all the crumbs are gone, Clare. I am reduced to feed birds now—I used to feed the poor once."

"Your poor are not neglected, dear; we have thought of all of them."

"Yes? Nobody is missed for very long, for very long! I have had a letter from papa—it made me laugh so! It is written in print letters and easy words, as if having a fever made one a child again. I don't believe he is coming home."

"Not coming home?"

"No. They tell me George Sylvester is here every day. George loves me, Janet and Carr love me, you love me—but I have loved two people in my life more than any of you: papa and Paul—does either of them love me as well? I want to see George, but I have a presentiment that he will cry—tell him he *must* not, for I cannot bear it. Mrs. Leslie-Gooch calls him a *feeling* young man, a sensible heart. I like *her*—she is kind and firm. We don't say *No* to her, Clare; she is despotic, I can tell you!" There was a girlish mischief in this confession that amused me, and the descriptive trait was true enough. I myself did not venture to say *No* to Mrs. Leslie-Gooch when she intimated that Felicia must rest from talking, and I must go away.

For several months Felicia made no perceptible advance from the condition in which I thus saw her. She continued languidly alive, and not much more than that. When the quite warm days came, Janet and Carr used to carry her downstairs to the summer parlour, or into the flower garden, where she was drawn about in a wheeled chair. That was a wonderful year for roses, and the roses at the Manor were famous. The sweet old Devoniensis was a pet of Felicia's, and she would make Janet fill her lap with the blossoms. Her love for flowers amounted to a passion, and her sense of the beautiful in nature was as lively as ever. To all else she was passive. That her father did not come was felt, no doubt, as a disappointment, but she never complained of his absence. When her grandmamma appeared, she was not more glad to see her than any other visitor. If her Uncle Tom and Rosy came, she was just as resigned and indifferent to them. She liked widow Burt to bring her boy, and set him toddling on the grass as much as anything, unless it was to have Sir Bevis by her chair, his muzzle on her knees, and his eyes on her face.

"Sir Bevis and George must be akin," she said one day; "they give so much devotion, and ask for nothing again."

George was her most frequent visitor, and if, for a few days, he did not come, she missed him. He used to tell her the Indian news. She had asked him for it in the first instance, and since that time he had not failed to read up all that might interest her. The name of Captain Gresham was not evaded by either—*he* was the pith of the Indian news, in fact.

Once and once only did I see Felicia give way to tears in the presence of a common acquaintance. It was during a visit from Miss Colquhoun, who could not refrain from offering a word in season—which meant a *sermonette*, delivered with closed eyes and a voice of grating monotony, upon the goodness of God in laying His hand of affliction upon her. The first check to her fluency was a sob from the patient, and an exclamation that it was easier to believe in the goodness of God when she was happy than it was now. Miss Colquhoun reclosed her eyes and redoubled her energy, threatening her with the certainty of more and more judgments if she refused to learn humility.

"Let them come, then!" retorted Felicia. "What have I left to lose that can compare with what I have lost already? I am so poor and forlorn a creature, that I may defy God to cast me lower than I am!"

Miss Colquhoun shrank back amazed and terrified—how sorry I was to hear such wild words from my darling! I entreated the tiresome woman to go away; but no, if she *could* find a word sharp enough to pierce to Felicia's soul, she *must* not lose her opportunity. I will not recite what she said; it was sadly injudicious and inappropriate.

"Oh! be still, and leave me to God!" cried Felicia, at last, and broken with fatigue, she fell a-weeping. Then Miss Colquhoun grew tender and tearful too. She hoped she had achieved a salutary impression, and went away humbly self-satisfied, with a promise to renew her visit shortly. But Mrs. Leslie-Gooch, when she witnessed the depressing effect of this, charged the servants not to admit her any more without a special permission.

Rosy Bethell too, in a timid, ineffectual way, would endeavour to give her cousin spiritual instruction. To her Felicia listened with good-humoured indulgence, allowing her what merit there might be in her intentions, but occasionally turning her reproach back upon herself.

"You are too presumptuous, Rosy; are you never afraid when you undertake to interpret the oracles of God?" I once heard her say. "What do you *know?* It would become you to learn, I think, before you teach. Nothing that you preach is the fruit of your own experience—it is just the beaten, grainless chaff of other people's. If I am all wrong, God is able to bring me to a right mind when He pleases, and I can wait. He fulfils Himself in so many ways, that I don't despair of His giving me a sort of moonlight happiness, when I have passed through my tribulations. It is nonsense to pretend that the disappointments, miseries, and disgraces that are befalling me are God's doings—they are your father's, and my father's, and grannie's, and I know not whose besides."

"Your own, dear Cousin Felicia."

"My own? Well, so be it! Cousin Clare calls me to blame, but you don't mean exactly the same thing. Others are selfish and cruel, and I am weak—and the weakest always go to the wall. 'I acknowledge my fault, and my sin is ever before me!' Whether I shall be a better woman for my troubles I cannot tell, but I shall be wiser—as the world counts wisdom. I shall have no more perfect faith in any one, and least of all in myself."

"He that trusteth in his own heart is a fool," quoth Rosy, and thought, no doubt, her quotation very apt.

It was a frequent expression on Felicia's lips now that her *faith* was gone—that trusting simplicity of goodness which had been such a charm of hers! But what wonder! She had despised and rejected the love that should have been more precious to her than life, and she had her reward in the neglect of her father, for whose release and profit she had been herself untrue. All through this summer, he never once came to see her; he excused himself on the plea of the uselessness of putting himself to pain—never considering whether or no his absence was putting her to greater pain. Then, her heir, greedy to enjoy a little earlier the power of her fortune, had conspired to make believe that she was mad, and had succeeded further than we yet knew. And since sickness had robbed her of strength and beauty, her friends in the world had fallen away from her and forgotten her—and her nearest in blood had set the world the example. If she came out of her affliction with a bitterness, sarcasm and defiance of spirit that had not distinguished her character before, was there any marvel in it? For her own peace sake I wished it had not been so, but it was too natural to complain of. This new, easy, tolerant contempt of herself and everybody else might last or it might not. Arthur and George said they did not know her with her false airs of being wise—they liked her ignorance better. But she had forfeited it: could she ever again love and trust as she had loved and trusted? They looked for impossibilities who expected it!

"I shall live, Cousin Clare, and shall most likely recover health enough to do my duty in life; and such as life will be, I mean to make the best of it," she said to me. "When papa does come home, I shall devote myself to his service like what he calls a 'reasonable' person. I have paid dear to keep it, but it is all I have, and it behoves me to cherish what has been so costly; his friends shall be my friends, and his pleasures my pleasures; and if I become, in time, what you don't quite like or approve, you and Arthur, then pity me, and say, I was meant originally to be of the better sort of womankind, but that circumstances were against me——"

I shall never forget the wistful, deprecating face with which she spoke these words—prophetic words, as one might well foresee! I know nothing more sad for a woman of noble nature than such a conscious acceptation of a lower lot than she was made for. They were farewell words too, and she added no more. She was at the Rectory gate in the carriage, to go away, when she spoke them, and they made an echo in my ears long after the echo of the wheels had died beyond the hill!

Mrs. Leslie-Gooch, Janet and Carr, and the old coachman were of her company. She was going to wander hither and thither as the fancy took her, travelling in her own carriage, with her little household, and stopping to rest when she was tired. This was her own plan, and nobody cared to oppose it. September was come, and they were to make first for the sea.

"Very crotchety of Felicia when there are railways everywhere, but it is best to indulge her fantastic humours: she is very odd and unsafe still, papa thinks," was a public comment of Rosy Bethell's upon her cousin's travelling arrangements. She made the remark at Archdeacon Colquhoun's in the midst of a party of morning-callers, and with indignant gravity I repudiated her insinuation on the spot.

"Rosy, I assure *you*, and everyone who hears us, that Felicia *never* was *odd* or *unsafe* in the sense you would convey, and it is abominable that all of you at Ringwood should persist in making-believe a lie."

"If Felicia never was *odd* and is not *odd* now, why should she be under the supervision of Dr. Gooch and Dr. Tuke, and actually in charge of their sister? Can you answer me that, Mrs. Gower?" cried Rosy, with an air of defiance.

"I will answer you nothing, Rosy. I am a witness of the truth, and dare to tell you that when you assert the cruel, malicious slander which your father and Miss Reed conspired to prove, you wilfully promote the lie of their inventing. They were defeated. Those two physicians pronounced your cousin no more mad than themselves or her accusers; they were her friends in that dreadful peril, a peril you have no conception of, and she has retained them for her protectors since——"

"An instance of remarkable courage and wisdom, I call it," said Miss Falkner, one of the persons present. "If her enemies array against her all the mad-doctors in the kingdom besides, Tuke and Gooch will confound their politics, baffle their knavish tricks, and save Miss Barrington!"

Everybody laughed except myself; I was too earnest and too much hurt. As for Rosy, she stuck to her papa's text, tossed her foolish little head consequentially, and informed us that there were "*Two sides to every story.*"

CHAPTER IV.

LETTERS IN ABSENCE.

FROM the September day when Felicia left the Manor in quest of the health-restoring tonic of change, I saw her no more until within a few weeks of her coming of age in the following June. But I had news of her, both by letter and by friends, and the shortest way to summarize the events which connect the two periods of her history will be to give some of her letters. The first that I shall quote is dated in October, from Aspencliff, a south-coast village that I had never heard of until I heard from her there.

"We are in the last days of summer, dear Clare, but its going is less perceptible here by the sea than amongst our oak and beech groves. I have had great peace since we came into this place, which the world has not found out yet; where there is only one thatched inn, and a few cottage-lodgings, where the butcher calls but once a week, and you may walk a mile on the shore without meeting a soul except the natives—amphibious beings who get their living on the sea. We have a cottage to ourselves—I try to make out the history of the people it belongs to; they are sisters, one is an invalid, and they have gone to Nice to see if the climate will cure her. They have left their home just as they live in it—sketches on the walls, books in their shelves, faded photographs, and brilliant illuminated texts—I occupy the invalid sister's room, and strange to say, *she* is not the pious one. '*Be the day weary or be the day long, It ringeth at last to even song,*' is the legend my eyes rest on when I sit in her reclining chair. It is a low-ceiled room with two peep-holes of dormer-windows in the thatch, and the scarlet glory of a Virginia creeper all bright about them in the sun to-day—another frost, a rain, a wind, and it will be gone! It was rash, perhaps, but the place caught my fancy, and all in a moment, I agreed to rent the cottage for the winter. That week with us at Hastings was enough for papa—by this time he is at Mentone. Mrs. Leslie-Gooch has begun a collection of sea-weeds. I have done nothing profitable but *bask*—my strength returns—I begin to like to walk better than to sit indoors; and to realize that, as grannie used to say, our life has other chapters besides its love-chapter. I go on turning the leaves."

"No, I shall not return to Gladeshire for my Cousin Blanche's wedding—how could I show my death's head at such a feast? She invites me to be her bridesmaid—*me*—when she has half-a-dozen pretty sisters, and Mr. Courtney one or two. George Sylvester, it seems, has declined Uncle Tom's invitations lately, and an invitation to the wedding in particular. Rosy says I am the cause, and calls me dog-in-the-manger. Poor Rosy, if George wished it, they should be welcome to my blessing to-morrow! But George has registered a vow that he will never marry while I am single—can I help his vows, foolish, fond fellow? He is in Essex just now, putting his fine Manor House in order, to go and reside there. We shall miss him from Bylands, but he does well to live on his own estate.

"Did you read the death of Mr. Jonathan Gresham in yesterday's *Times?* It mentioned that he had only survived his brother six weeks. What a change in Captain Gresham's fortunes! When he comes home it will be as master of Fairfield, and inheritor of his uncles' wealth. His sister Kitty did not love me very much, but I hope she and her boys will have a share. Does grannie ever speak of him and me as if she were sorry?"

"One of the chief reasons why I liked Aspencliff when first we came was for the sake of its church, and its old clergyman; he looked so holy, so mild and benevolent, that it was a comfort only to see and hear him! He did not call upon us, and last Sunday, to my dismay, a stranger was in his place, and we were told that the rector had gone away for three months. The place has lost its charm—don't be surprised if my next news is that we are gone too."

"I have very little to write about—the days are dull, the nights are long, and my night-thoughts are heavy. What a melancholy moan there is from the sea! We are at Dawlish, but one place is much the same as another to the weary-hearted; we must carry our sunshine with us or we have none.

"What a blessed little woman you are, Cousin Clare, with your beloved Arthur, and Jack and Tinykins! I wonder whether many women are such fools as I am! I should dearly like to have a little child of my own—I fancy sometimes that I am pressing one to my heart, loving it, kissing it, as you love Tinykins. And it will never be any more than a dream-child! Who was it wrote of his Dream-Children? I should like to read it—ask Arthur if he knows whose book it is in.

"Sophie Christianson announces her engagement—so does Jenny Sylvester, and both cry: 'Come to my wedding!' I will have nothing to do with their weddings, I tell them—I am envious, and gloomy, and in mourning for my own lost love.

"Grandmamma Barrington wants me to go to Hampton Court; it would be unkind to refuse, yet I would rather not go—I have been so happy there; I dread the sight of the river, and the beautiful rides in the Park. I often think—does Paul remember? Shall we ever meet again, and if we meet, how will it be? Do you hear if he is to come home? the mutiny is crushed, and the war at an end. But why do I ask? What is he to me? What am I to him? Still we may acknowledge an interest in the person we have once loved—it was not by our own fault we were thrust asunder."

"I wish sometimes that I could cease from thinking of Paul, of the past, of what made and still makes me so unhappy. For there is no good in it, and the present is darker and more difficult for those shadows. I don't want to spend all my life regretting. But let it be! Time will do for me, perhaps, what by no effort can I do for myself."

"Cousin Rosy has written me a full account of Blanche's wedding, which event went off delightfully. She consults me also on her own affairs, and I do not feel competent to counsel her. She has had a series of little fancies, but never a great passion, and, as she frankly confesses, never one offer, pretty face and pretty fortune notwithstanding! She *likes* George Sylvester now, but she would like anybody else, with the same advantages, equally well to-morrow—for it is a mistake to suppose that Rosy's spirituality has attained to the renunciation of the pomps and vanities of the world yet. I don't remember that she ever did anything but laugh at George while his heirship hung in doubt—and I could tell her, if it were worth while, that George does not like her—she talks too much for him. Being such a chatterbox, no doubt all the neighbourhood is in her confidence by now—what do *you* think of her idea of leaving Ringwood, and setting up house *à la Colquhoun*, with Miss Reed for her companion? She is Uncle Tom's favourite of all his children, but with the second edition of girls grown and growing up, the household has too many mistresses to be very harmonious. Poor old Reed, for her sins, has been toiling and troubling amongst the younger children since she left the Manor, doing the duties of nursery-governess; and even in that capacity, where she must earn her living hardly enough, and be perfectly effaced as to importance in the family, Mrs. Bethell cannot tolerate her. Rosy is nearly seven-and-twenty, and her income is quite enough for easy independence—I wish I had been born to no more, and then I might have been happy in my own way, with a love of my own choice! I imagine that Rosy's scheme originated with poor Reed, who must long to exchange her turbulent school-room for another mild companionship. Blanche's marriage was the occasion of Amy's 'coming-out,' and Dulcy is to make her *début* at the next Hunt Ball—not one of those girls but has a charming face; the third, Mabel, is the beauty of all, Rosy says. Lucky for them that they are handsome, for what a family Uncle Tom has—seven girls and six boys, counting Rosy and Blanche. I shall not be sorry to hand him over the share he stipulated for as the condition of breaking the entail of the Yorkshire property to settle papa's affairs next June—those boys will take some putting-out in the world. Tom and Frank go in and out from Ringwood to the Grammar School at Gladestone every day. I have offered to charge myself with Bobby's education (he is my godson, you know). His father and mother would have liked me to take Tom instead, and to give him an Eton training, but Tom is no favourite of mine, and Bobby is my own boy, in a fashion. How proud I was to stand for him, when I was only twelve years old myself! The christening was at the Manor—do you recollect? Dear mamma was living then.—I hope you will be satisfied with this letter—I *do* try to create myself interests beyond the narrow round of my own feelings, and, in a measure, I succeed. With this goes to the post a cheque for Bobby's tailor. Bobby is just promoted to a suit of boy's clothing—sailor-blue trousers, jacket, and vest—I longed to drop a golden tip into his first pocket!—is that practical enough for you, little Jack's mother?"

"Grannie Barrington does not *say* anything, but I read in her face, the moment we met, how much she saw me altered. I suppose it was the fever burnt away my beauty—I *was* beautiful *once*, Clare, eh? I remember it with more vanity than I ever felt in its possession—will it return? It is from Janet I receive the discipline worst, and she, dear soul, lays on the lash quite unconsciously! 'No, Miss Felicy, a bit of colour, a black velvet band—all white is *so* trying to the complexion; you did use to wear it *formerly*, but——' a woeful sigh makes a full stop. Janet's *formerly* sounds such a dreary long way behind us!

"Uncle Ralph is here, and as cynical as ever. He was astonished to find me looking so much like myself after what he had heard. I asked him *what* he had heard, but he only rejoined with a tirade on female curiosity, and declined to tell me. Merry or melancholy, Clare, we are an untiring source of interest to ourselves! It would do me no good to hear the gossip that has gone the round of our world concerning me, and yet I should *like* to hear it."

"'Black as ash-buds in March!' The ash-buds are black, and so it is March again. More than a year and a half ago!

"Next month papa is to be in London, and I am to join him—we have not our own house, you know, and we shall not remain for the season, but he has promised that I shall be with him somewhere. Till then I stay with grannie, and willingly, because I am of some use and comfort to her. I often meet my ghosts, but they don't scare me. Once I thought to exorcise them, but they are stronger than I, and will haunt me all the days of my life—perhaps, I should be lonelier at heart without them!

"Mrs. Leslie-Gooch has another appointment: the care of an unfortunate lady in much the same condition as poor Mrs. Cholmondeloy of Heathburn was.—Ah! Clare, if I *had* been mad! but except in the delirium of my fever, there was never an hour when I was not conscious of each pang I suffered, and as well aware of the past, the present and the future as any of you about me. It was cruel to say and do what they did; but, perhaps, they believed my mind was gone.

"Miss Sophie Christianson has been down for two days. She did her best to provoke me to sing, but I could not find my voice. She will live in London after her marriage—an arrangement imperatively necessary for her welfare. Even papa does not more loathe the monotonous, innocent pleasures of a country life than my sprightly friend. I have *half* pledged myself to take some singing-lessons from her master when I am in town; he is a prodigious genius, she avers, but awfully poor, and beaten at all points by envy and jealousy in his attempts to make his way; he is German, and only a year in London yet, a new beginner. I used to rejoice in the music of my voice once, and I suppose it is ther still, if the spirit would awake that used to touch its chords."

"Uncle Ralph carried me to town yesterday for an interview with Cannon and Vigors; and on leaving their offices, who should I meet in the same dull lawyers' quarter but Mrs. Willis, accompanied by her elder boy. There was a moment's hesitation whether we should shake hands, or pass with a formal recognition, but she made a distinct halt, and the little boy called out my name, and there we were confronting one another. The colour rose in my face and in hers too, and what we said by way of politeness perhaps neither of us recollects. I felt painfully confused, and she gazed at me with that mingled surprise and compassion which I read in all eyes seeing me for the first time since my illness. Her news was that she was leaving Bylands, and going to reside at Harrow for the education of her boys; the munificence of her bachelor-uncles having made such an education their right. Her mother, she said, had died quite suddenly at Fairfield—there had been no time even to telegraph to Bylands for her. What a mother she was! living without love for her children, and dying without care for them! All in her power she bequeathed to her husband, nothing to her daughter—fortunately Fairfield was hers only for life. Kitty avoided her brother's name, and I would not be the first to mention it, though I burned to ask if he were returning to England soon.

"A purchaser has been found for the Yorkshire property in Sir Guy Vaux, and Cannon and Vigors have all in train to conclude the sale directly they receive the necessary powers. Papa impatiently expects the day that shall make him a free agent once more. How are we to celebrate my coming of age? Ask grannie what was done at mamma's majority—that shall be the precedent for mine."

"Have you observed a mysterious paragraph that is going the round of the papers, concerning a certain noble duke of mature years, who is about to form a second matrimonial alliance with a lady of rank, one of the most distinguished beauties of the day? Papa told me the interpretation thereof this morning—by noon it will be all over the town; but it ought to be quite fresh news for you to promulgate in the country to-morrow. Make it a calling-day, and you will be a windfall of gossip for your friends!—The noble duke is *our* duke, the distinguished beauty is the Honourable Miss Pemberton; *he* is sixty-two, *she* is twenty-six, and very handsome, indeed. I asked papa how Lady Augusta liked the marriage. 'Oh,' he said, 'she is perfectly well pleased with it'—which astounds me! They are abroad, and the marriage is to be performed at the British Embassy in Paris—papa seemed to know all about it. You will have heard that the Marquis is moribund? The doctors say that there is brain disease of long standing, and that he has not been always as responsible for his acts as other men. Poor fellow, with what an antipathy, what a sense of loathing, he inspired me!

"Papa is in his most genial humour—no one is pleasanter than he when he gives his mind to it! His deliverance draws nigh, and I have reasonable grounds of confidence that his two years of bondage may have taught him a salutary caution against play. These apartments are not very commodious, but they are cheerful, with sun all day, when it shines. The back-drawing-room is our dining-room, and our round table sees two or three guests every night. Mr. and Mrs. Mellish have been amongst them, and Jack Colquhoun, my aversion; but they went at ten, like other people, and so far as I know, papa has not touched a card or a billiard-cue since he came to London.

"I have begun my lessons with Sophie Christianson's German master. There is still one fount of joy left me in life, and that is music! I will not tell you what he says of my voice, but since I broke silence, I have hardly ceased singing except to eat and sleep. Janet stands listening at the door, and crying—she says my voice is as much changed as my face, but for the better instead of the worse:—indeed, I know myself, that it has a sweet depth of expression it could not have before, because then I sang without love's thorn in my breast. Oh! Clare, how much more one can sing than one can say!"

"Yesterday papa and I went to a morning amateur concert at Kingston House—the first crowd I have been in yet. It was an ordeal, but he entreated: 'To please *me*, Felicia;' so Janet got me up beautifully, I called my courage to aid, and we set off. Mrs. Mellish was to sing, and she asked us to take her in our carriage—I used not to be self-conscious, Cousin Clare, but it seemed to me, when we entered those splendid rooms, that all heads turned, and all eyes stared our way. Mrs. Mellish is a pet with the *habitués* of Kingston House, and she was instantly surrounded, and carried off to the orchestra. I felt rather alone, for I saw no one whom I knew. However, papa stayed by me, people settled into their places, and the concert began.

"You remember how music bears me away, what ecstasy of pleasure is in it—I had forgotten the crowd and myself, and all things that annoy, when there was Sophie's German at my ear (in whose behalf the concert was given) earnestly supplicating my help:—one of the singers had failed him, and there was only myself who could fill her place—it was for a song of his own composing, which I had practised with him. Mrs. Mellish, Sophie, the host came to add their petition to his; papa whispered: 'Go, Felicia, don't disappoint the poor fellow—it is *the* song of the concert;' and a second glance at my master's face, lean with privation, and pale with tremor, made it easier to consent than to refuse.

"I sang the song with him—it was a duet—once, twice, *thrice*—they encored us a second time. Think of *that!* but it is, indeed, a lovely song, and will make his fortune. He seemed as if he would fall on his knees in his fervour of gratitude. What intoxication there is in success and applause! We sang our song better the second time than the first, and best of all the third, and I should not have refused to sing again—*I*, who, an hour before, quaked to go in amongst the fashionable mob! *Ce n'est que le premier pas qui coûte.*

"To-day poor Max has been to renew his thanks,

and to ask me to accept the dedication of his song; for which he has found a publisher eager already. The Kingston House set are very exclusive; 'all the talents' are welçome, and the standard of morals is not *too* high, lest any should be shut out. I shall have the *entrée* for a song, while my novelty lasts.—Grannie Bethell's axioms prove themselves true one after another. Our happiness gone, we take up easily with pleasure; and dance to its will-o'-the-wisps until—until they lead us into sloughs of despond, eh, Clare? or until the dawn of a new morning?

"However it be in the end, I have the present satisfaction of pleasing papa. I never knew him in more excellent humour."

"Why are you sorry, dear Clare, that I should be 'one of them' at Kingston House? The excitement of society carries me away for but a very little while; when I leave the lights, the flowers, the music, the conversation, and am shut up in my room, I am like a bow unstrung. I recognize the vanity and emptiness of all things, philosophy included, but I must live my life! If papa is to be my comrade, I must study him. He hates such simple tastes as I have cultivated—he does not care to hear me sing when we are alone; but it is his pride and delight to hear my praises when I sing for other people. *He* studies *me* as he never did before—asks me what I wish to do, where I wish to go, even postpones his engagements to mine; takes notice of my looks, my dress, tells me what suits me best, and what does not become me—is almost as attentive as a lover! Don't laugh at me, Clare, you cannot conceive how painful was his neglect, and more than neglect, a year or two ago. And what touches me most of all with the sense of kindness restored is, that he talks of the dear old Manor as our home together—our home where he intends us to be together more than in the years past. I wish we may, Oh, I wish we may! And if he endure its quiet, for my sake, surely, for the few weeks we are in town, I ought to be gay for his. Comradeship has its duties, dear Clare; all the indulgence and all the forbearance cannot be on one side.—However, I have declined any part in the private theatricals; I should not make a good actress; so papa and I will only go to Kingston House on Saturday as two of the audience."

"This is the third time our descent upon Stoneleigh is deferred, but we really *are* to come home next week (just as London is beginning to fill). I, at least, shall come, even if papa stay behind; probably he will beg a little longer law, and I must not hold the reins *too* tight.—Whoever has reported to you that I acted in the comedy at Kingston House has been misinformed. I did not appear upon the stage at all; I only sang a *soubrette's* song that had to be sung behind the scenes, the lady who took the part not being able to sing. Nowhere in London can we meet so many celebrities as at Kingston House. The *conversaziones* there are famous; even you, dear little countrywoman, who suspect something wicked in whatever is gay and pleasant, might attend them with advantage. The names of men and women most distinguished in art and literature are familiar there, and oh! the disappointments that sometimes we encounter! Your pet poetess has a visage which announces the most practical character. The modern Hannah More, who indites her moralities with such muddy ink, is a frowsy old person, and affects youth and fashion in her dress. You know the exquisite little memorial chapel to the late duchess, at Lowndes—the great genius who built it looks like a dissipated, consequential, bumptious cock-robin. You have a too pathetic engraving in your bed-room, it moves one to tears to see it—the painter of the original is a shrewd Scotchman, overflowing with anecdote, who has an immense bushy black head, and a rosy, weather-tanned, jovial countenance; and the painter who has achieved the widest popular success, and perhaps made the most money of any artist living, has an air of weary disgustful indifference to his notoriety, as if he had found himself out a sham, and despised the world for not finding him out too.—You ask me if the famous folk admire themselves excessively. No—the more sense, the more simplicity. I have heard tales of the envies and jealousies said to exist amongst the stars of the first magnitude, but I don't believe a tithe of what I hear. It is a theory of mine that each knows his own place, and forms a more true estimate of his work than his keenest critic, and that herein lies his root of discontent or of hope, as his case may be. The 'Modern Hogarth,' for instance, as he is universally bepraised—what gives him his face of tired indifference to *fame*, as we call the appreciation which makes rich? He is well-liked, he is kind, he has hosts of friends, he has a fine family of sons and daughters, and a devoted help-meet; there is no failure of dexterity in his hand, no dulness yet in his conceptions; it would be a bold word to utter at Kingston House in this generation, that his pictures are shallow, vulgar, and will not last. But *he* knows it—he knows that he cannot touch Hogarth when Hogarth rises to the full height of his power.—Portraits are to me ever the most interesting pictures in old collections, and there is one portrait-painter often at Kingston House whose portraits might hang besides those of Rembrandt. I don't like the man, but I like his work. He is not at all run after, perhaps he will never be found out, save by a few, while he is living, but he is *sure* of his crown after the strifes and envyings of posterity are laid at rest.—It would be a consolation to know that ghosts revisit the earth, if only that the ghosts of the disappointed might see how coolly posterity upsets the verdicts of the infallibles who had the dispensing of favour and patronage while they walked in the flesh.

"What a long letter I have written you with my own hand! It should convince you that I have opened my ears to my counsellors; that I am mending my ways, getting out of my groove, giving my mind to the world, and the things and people of the world. It is better so—is it not?

"Farewell. Expect no more news until we meet."

CHAPTER V.

HYDRA.

THE gradual change of tone in Felicia's letters prepared me to find a change also in herself, but not such a change as there actually was. She came upon me in the garden one May evening, without warning, having just arrived at the Manor: a fashionable fine lady, gay, laughing, even a little loud and excited. She took me by the chin and kissed me, called me names of rural simplicity—but I was not deceived; there was as much nervousness as reality about her; this new manner which transformed my darling was as much put on as her bonnet! She looked well in the face, was fuller in figure than formerly, a woman quite, and a very lovely woman.

Arthur saw us from the study-window, and came out—then Jack, then Tiny, all the family to greet and welcome her. But the glee of the event was gone in a moment; for she scarcely noticed the children. They ran off, Arthur fell behind, and she began to say: "Well, Cousin Clare, you have not told me yet how I strike you. I expected to see hands cast up in amazement, to hear shouts of joyful congratulation, and you seem hardly to know me. Am I then so strange?"

I made haste to re-assure her; for there was a wistful expression in her eyes as if she were hurt and disappointed. It occurred to me that, perhaps, she believed she looked quite her girlish self again, had an ardent desire that it should be so, had been told by others that it was, but waited its confirmation from me, who had not been witness to the slow stages of her recovery in her eight months' absence. Whether she was satisfied with my answer was not easy to tell; she smiled, looked on the ground, then up at the great oaks, and said with a suppressed sigh that nothing was altered about our placid parsonage; with a kind afterthought she spoke of the little ones, turned to see if Arthur were still near, and then asked if there was anything fresh in the village.

The nimble tongues of both of us were made slow because neither wished to be the first to speak of what was uppermost in her thoughts. However, it was impossible to part even for an hour until we had told the burden on our minds. Felicia was still in her travelling dress, dusty after her journey, and pressed to be gone; for her Cousin Rosy awaited her, having arrived from Ringwood that afternoon, on her own proposal to be her cousin's companion till Mr. Barrington came down.

With a sudden warm suffusion of her face Felicia halted near the gate as we walked to and fro the lawn, and said straight out: "I have heard that Paul is in England—is he at Fairfield?"

"Yes, he has been there some weeks. Helen has seen him."

"Has he written to you, Clare? I thought, perhaps, he might have written to you."

"No. Helen says he is wonderfully strong and

brown, older, more manly, and that he has let his beard grow, which gives him quite a grand air."

"Do you know whether he intends to live at Fairfield?"

"Yes. He told Helen he meant to keep the place up, and to have his sister there."

That was all that was said. Felicia kissed me again with a little shiver, and a remark that it was still cold in the evenings, and then I walked across to the Manor with her, and came back alone.

It was impossible but that certain hopes, chances, probabilities should suggest themselves to Felicia as to me, but we kept them secretly in our own bosoms. I may say *now* what mine were. I reflected that Captain Gresham was in England, was free, had been singularly favoured by fortune in his absence, was become a match for any girl in the county, be she heiress, or titled, or ever so beautiful. His return home, almost coincident with Felicia's coming of age, was not, I thought, accidental. In another month she would be her own mistress; and if he chose to renew his suit, and she to accept it, there was literally *no* reason why she should not claim to be released from her rash vow, and let the past be retrieved.

Yet while I was able to establish these facts most conclusively to my own mind, all the while I had a foreboding that they would not turn as I wished. Helen confided to me that Captain Gresham, while in India, had been kept regularly posted up in all that was happening at the Manor, and even in all the most exaggerated and false reports that issued from Ringwood. She told me that he gave himself no airs of sentimental regret, and had much more the appearance of a stout soldier who had roughed it in hard service, and was ready to rough it again, than of a lover longing to sit at his lady's feet: — in short, Helen's opinion was that his passion for Felicia had become extinct, and that it would not be resuscitated. She believed that he would rather avoid than seek Felicia now, and said it was a pity that I should encourage her to think any longer of him tenderly. I did not encourage her or discourage her. I neither said nor did any thing for which I can blame myself. I just waited, watching what time and opportunity might do; for I had my own opinion whether Captain Gresham's love for my darling was dead or not. Of one circumstance, perhaps, I did not make enough account—and that is, of the influence upon his feelings and imagination of the fables told him concerning Felicia—it never occurred to me that he might be disenchanted, and his passion chilled into pity.

He was at Fairfield and she at Stoneleigh, only a couple of hours' ride apart, and yet he made no effort to see her that I am aware of. She was exceedingly restless and unsettled for a day or two, constantly expecting him, perhaps; but when the week drew to an end, and he made no sign, she gave that up, and all her talk was of her papa's coming, and of the guests she meant to assemble at the Manor for the celebration of her majority. Lady Augusta, she informed me with proud satisfaction, poor deluded girl, was to stay in the house; the Mellishes were asked especially to please her papa; and especially to please herself,

George Sylvester; and Sophie, her newly-married friend, delivered from the paternal despotism, was to come with her more indulgent master and spouse, Mr. Cardigan.

A ball was to crown the festivities, to which half the county was bidden. Felicia and Rosy were filling up the cards of invitation one afternoon when I went in to hear how they progressed; and said Rosy, without looking up from her task, in the coolest, matter-of-fact tone: "Shall I address one to Fairfield?"

"Keep to your own list, Rosy, or we shall be sending two to some houses, and leaving others out altogether, and so we shall give offence," replied Felicia, not lifting her head either.

"A good many people will be disappointed if they don't meet Captain Gresham," Rosy continued, whether for cruelty or pure dulness of apprehension I could not determine.

Felicia did not answer her, but her face burnt. If she was in any perplexity how to act, which I do not imagine she was, Captain Gresham relieved her of it himself; for Mrs. Claylands coming in while she was thus busy, said, in the course of conversation, that her son Tom was going across to Ireland with Captain Gresham the next day, and she was afraid Tom would not be back for Felicia's ball. Neither of the young men was back until the gossip over that event was giving place to other news of even more general and particular interest; but their absence did not appear to excite any public regret, for the festivities at the Manor went off without a flaw.

Short memories are convenient in society. It was not two years yet since Felicia Barrington's broken engagement had made a nine-days' talk in town and country; but so far as I could tell, everybody had forgotten it, or thought it so long-ago and done-for an affair, that they might discuss Fairfield and its master before her with perfect good taste, and she hear them with perfect equanimity. Perhaps it did not enter into anybody's dreams but my own that the engagement could possibly be renewed. Captain Gresham had been transformed from a "detrimental" into a man of wealth and consideration. The deepest and liveliest interest of mothers with daughters to marry centred on Fairfield. The daughters had always adored him, and now the matrons adored him too, and Fairfield was at this epoch the favourite theme in boudoirs and on ball-room benches.

And at the same time much of the romance that had shed its light about Felicia three or four years ago, when she bloomed upon the world in all the freshness of youth, a complete beauty, accomplished, charming, good, was dimmed and faded. It struck me with a sense of vext pain and compassion to observe how, in her own house, on the day when she was taking possession of her birthright, she was not the *first*. And she was conscious of it. She had lost much of the calm, easy self-confidence of her happy days, and though she made a splendid figure at night in the ball-room, wearing her diamonds and a dress of rose-coloured satin and Brussels point, Lady Augusta overshadowed her with a magnificent, graceful dignity; and her little cousin, Mab Bethell, outshone her in the lustrous, dewy loveliness, which is the magic of a girl.

Pretty little Mab! she was the third girl from Ringwood (Rosy had retired from the dancing category), and her two elder sisters tried eloquently to prove that she ought not to go to Felicia's ball —she was not *out*, she was not fifteen, she was not in long dresses, she did not know how to behave—but Mab with that sweet, frank courage which conquers fortune, appealed to her Cousin Felicia against them all; and Felicia, ever kind, to make sure of her not being disappointed, brought her off to the Manor three days before, gave her a white net dress, starred with gold, to make a fairy-queen of her, and everybody, I think, old and young, man and woman, declared her to be, for beauty, the Queen of the Ball. I recollect the clusters of pleased, admiring faces that watched her dancing, and I know that mine was one. Such delicious, innocent, provoking ways she had! She knew herself a pet, and lovely. She read it in all eyes, and indulgence on all lips; and so it came to pass that after the great ball at the Manor, it was Mab we heard extolled, and not Felicia—Mab who was talked of most, and not the heiress come to her kingdom.

No, I must except George Sylvester. He was loyal and constant to his early playmate, his first and only love—*he* would not admit that Mab was anything to wonder at in comparison with Felicia. Pretty! to be sure she was pretty—every girl was pretty if she pleased! He dared to say this to Rosy who challenged his opinion—*she* beginning to take the affectionate pride of an elder sister, past rivalry, in Mab.

Rosy was scorny on the occasion, and said to me afterwards: "George Sylvester is quite infatuated still; the more Felicia will not care for him, the more humbly he worships her. If she ever *does* get married now, it will be George who will take her—a man of sense would think a good many times before he would run the risk that threatens *her*. I never see her walking with her chin in the air, and her great mournful eyes staring straight onward; as if her thoughts were a thousand miles away, without feeling afraid that she may go off again at any moment."

What is the name of that crawling worm which you may cut into a score of pieces, and every piece remain alive? It answers in nature to a big, malicious calumny in society. Here was that horrible Ringwood invention which I had struck, stamped on, crushed with all my might, rearing its ugly head to spit in my face again!

I kept down my indignation enough to say: "Rosy, I cannot make up my mind whether you are most silly or most wicked. But I am sure that you have a false tongue and one very hard spot, at least, in your heart, or you could not persist in repeating this cruel, this fatal slander on your cousin."

"I only repeat what papa says—what Miss Reed, who was with Felicia at the worst, would swear and substantiate in a court of justice any day. I heard her say as much to Mrs. Willis not a month ago."

"Swear it she might, substantiate it she most

assuredly would not against the testimony of Dr. Tuke and Dr. Gooch in Felicia's favour."

Rosy smiled superior. "Well, Mrs. Gower, I will not quarrel with you about it—hard words don't alter hard facts. We all know you are so bigoted in your friendship for Felicia that you would make out everybody a fool or a liar who does not believe in her to the same extent. Poor thing! I am *very* sorry for her. She has Stoneleigh, but I would not stand in her shoes to be put in possession of it to-morrow; and if George Sylvester marries her, weak, comfortable, easy-tempered fellow that he is, I don't envy him the distracted sort of marble wife she will make. Mrs. Mellish said to me only yesterday: 'Poor Miss Barrington, she is quite a bore, with her eternal sorrows and regrets!'"

I hated Mrs. Mellish for that speech—but she only spoke after her kind!

A series of pleasant entertainments—dinners and garden-parties chiefly—were given in the neighbourhood during the weeks that followed the ball at the Manor. The Duke and the new

Duchess came to Lowndes in the middle of June, there was the bustle of their reception in the county, and festivities to celebrate that. Felicia accepted every invitation with her father; but though Captain Gresham was once more at Fairfield, they never met.

At the end of the month she went for three days to the Castle with her father, and thence, without returning home, to London, to complete the sale of the Yorkshire estate. Mr. Tom Bethell went up to town at the same time to perform his promised part, and the lawyers being ready with the deeds, and Sir Guy Vaux with the purchase-money, the business was not long a-doing. Tom Bethell's share of the plunder was one-third—for so much he sold his chance of the reversion; the two-thirds over and above his spoil, sufficed to release Mr. Barrington from his long-accumulated debts and difficulties, and also from that fear of Tom Bethell which had acted as a prudent restraint on his expenses for the last two years.

Felicia received her father's grateful thanks:—

"Ah, papa," said she, "I wish your troubles had cost me no more than the money!"

A few days after she came home to the Manor alone, leaving Mr. Barrington still in London, on the plea of those mysterious affairs to transact, which such gentlemen as he, with nothing to do, commonly explain as "*business*."

CHAPTER VI.

A SURPRISE FOR THE WORLD.

IT did not impress me as a favourable out-look for the future, that so soon after his redemption Mr. Barrington should expose his daughter to remark upon his neglect of her; but nothing selfish in him surprised me.

A few days after her return to the country, Felicia sent to ask me to drive with her to the Dower House. She and her Grandmamma Bethell were on complacent terms again:—"We talk worldly philosophy one against the other; and she is flattered that I am become her disciple, and acknowledge her teaching to be true," said my darling, with that wistful air of indifference and hopelessness which was growing into her most marked characteristic.

Yet of some things she was scrupulously mindful—in evidence of it, I recall an incident of this day. As we passed Widow Burt's cottage, the old woman was at her gate, her grandson, now a stout boy, in her arms. The sight of them caused Felicia to speak of some provision she wished to make for the child, to be sure that her pledge to his mother should never be forfeited. "I want you to ask Mr. Gower," she said, "how and where I can place a little money in security for that boy, so that it would bring in enough to make it worth somebody's while to take care of him, if his grandmother should die before he is old enough to fend for himself. As for me, there is no telling what may happen. Nothing feels fast under my feet, and there are so many circumstances in which a woman cannot do what she would. Just at this moment I have a sum in hand of which I need render no one account, and I want to give it to the boy, out of my own power entirely, and without letting any of my people talk about it. While I was in London last with papa, I settled something with Cannon and Vigors, for Bobby Bethell, that he may get his commission when he is old enough, and be able to purchase his steps—I don't suppose I shall ever be so rich again in ready money, but it is a load off my heart to feel that, however foolishly I may guide my own life, I have done what I can to give them a good start."

I assured her of Arthur's assistance; she had it, and young Burt's 'prentice-fee to a cabinet-maker in Gladestone (the lad having chosen cabinet-making for his trade) was defrayed only last year out of the small fund she secured to him.

The dowager had not come to Felicia's ball, and I had not seen her for several months. All at once, she was becoming an old woman, her head had a palsied motion, and her hands were shaky, feeble and slow. Felicia's presence increased her tremulousness; she was evidently in fear of her—and who could marvel if conscience pricked her every time she saw her once pride and treasure? The changes in our friends made by sickness and trouble strike us anew on each occasion of seeing them, for the first time, in places where we have been used to see them familiarly in their health and prosperous content. As we sat in the pretty drawing-room, Felicia's figure was visible to me from head to foot, reflected in a long mirror—I could hardly recognize her: hair, dress, manner, countenance, complexion were so different! She was talking with much more animation, more action and gesture than she talked formerly:—

"Papa will stay in London as long as there is anybody to stay for; he has business there—you know what papa means when he says he has *business*. He is as light-hearted as ever! Will he come for the partridges? Oh, yes; for Lady Augusta has promised us another visit then."

"It appears that Lady Augusta is fond of the Manor;" remarked the dowager.

"Yes; she thinks it a charming old house, and quite envies me mamma's boudoir—her own room at the Castle has neither so beautiful a view, nor so many prettinesses of its own. Papa has exquisite taste—it was he who designed the oval window, and had the boudoir so elegantly fitted up for mamma."

"I recollect, and the expense was no trifle—it was *mine* before it was *hers;* now it is *yours;* and you have a right to the enjoyment of it, for the whole house is *yours,* and I hope I shall never hear of your giving it up to anybody," said the old lady, with a break in her voice.

"Give it up! to whom should I give it up?" cried Felicia amazed.

"If Lady Augusta is to be your frequent guest, you might be moved by politeness or good-nature to let her have it."

"And make myself a stranger in my own house! Oh, no! she would not think of it. There is a sitting-room adjoining the bed-room she has had before—we give her the maple-room, because there is a maid's room close at hand."

Mrs. Bethell made no rejoinder to this explanation, but her eyes rested for some moments on Felicia's face, as if she were considering some matter in her mind, and doubting whether to speak of it or not. Apparently she decided to hold her peace; for the subject was changed, and the ball was discussed.

"I hear of nothing but Mab Bethell—wild little monkey, full of mischief, that she was two years ago, and broke me a valuable china jar in her romps," said the dowager.

"Mab is very dear and sweet," replied Felicia, and her whole countenance brightened with the reflection of that spotless, cloudless, dawning life.

"You were far more beautiful, Felicia, once. I don't know why you have gone off so!"

"Perhaps it is because I have got out of the sunshine, grannie."

"Then, my dear, get into it again."

"I do—wherever I see a promise of warmth, thither I fly. You know Kingston House, that enclosed, perfumed society-garden? When I become acclimatized to its artificial heat, perhaps I shall bloom as brilliantly there as ever I did under the open sky."

"They are not quite the *best* set who frequent Kingston House, Felicy."

"Perhaps not, grannie, but they suit *me*. To live with Cousin Rosy, so righteous, so awfully superior as she is, feels like living in a church—

new, bleak, bare, pewed and very protestant. The *habitués* of Kingston House are as various as the kneeling throng in a Roman cathedral—a woman that is a sinner may go in amongst them without fear of being bidden to stand off, for they are holier than she."

"You are not a sinner in that sense, Felicia," said her grannie, reproachfully. "Why do you say such extraordinary things? A stranger might put I know not what construction on your words."

Felicia laughed with a sad irony. "God be merciful to us, miserable sinners! That is our Sunday confession—on week-days we are all good, kind, charitable souls—eh? Indeed, grannie, my heart condemns me! I dare not cast a stone at any neighbour I have as worse than myself; but there is always that red shade of Mephistopheles for a comforter, to whisper that there are none much better, let them carry their saintship ever so loftily!"

The palsied shaking of the dowager's head and hands was painful to witness, as she answered:

"I thought, my dear, that Mephistopheles was a tempter in the old play."

Felicia laughed that bitter laugh again, but she trembled too: her own daring, foolish words scared her; for she had been brought up to know and believe and do what is right. She felt my gaze dwelling on her with sorrow, and with a sudden impulse, leaning forward to me, she said in her natural voice: "There is somebody who never forgets to pray for me, Clare; and such prayers stay us from falling—don't they?"

"I have no fear for you, Felicia," said I. "We are none of us our own keepers; but God is near when we cry."

"Yes, yes," added the old lady most eagerly. "There is a promise in the Bible that as our day is, so shall our strength be; and another promise about a way of escape being given with every temptation. The Bible is a very good book, Felicia; your dear mamma was always fond of it—I hope you are fond of it too? You cannot read anything better when you are in distress. Miss Lassell's father was a clergyman, and she reads me a chapter every night and morning. I grow old—I have had many disappointments, and it behoves me to prepare for the great change that awaits us all."

Felicia rose from her seat, and kissed her tenderly: "Have you been disappointed in *me*, grannie? I am sorry;—but, you know, the greatest disappointments wear out if we live long, and in the grave all things are forgotten." And then she signed to me that we would go. Miss Lassells answered to a certain touch of the bell, and we left her.

"The tears of old people hurt me more than any," said my darling, as we were on our road home again. "And yet I do not think they suffer as acutely as we do—I hope they don't, for poor grannie's sake. Miss Lassells is very kind to her. But oh, Clare, what a tawdry bit of tapestry life looks, at last, if we have woven it all of our own absurd devices!"

"Yes," said I, taking up her metaphor, "and the mischief is, that one grotesque blunder does not save wilful weavers from another. They go on twisting and turning the thread about, and breaking it and piecing it, and being so *very* clever, that the original design is quite obscured or lost, and the finished toil is nothing better than a wrong side, or a bundle of loose ends."

"How many more grotesque blunders shall I be guilty of, Clare, before I have done my weaving?"

"Who can tell? You can hardly make a worse than the first, Felicia."

"So you think. But as I look onward to the years, I see vast possibilities in my life—a whole comedy of errors. And sometimes I take fright and wish myself at that bourn, whatever it be, whence no traveller returns—down in that silence where the wicked cease from troubling, and the weary are at rest!"

Rosy Bethell did not love her Cousin Felicia, and Felicia did not care for Rosy, but circumstances made it convenient that they should associate together. Felicia was much alone at the Manor, Rosy was a free agent (she had not left Ringwood yet, but her step-mamma was always glad to expedite her visits away from home), and thus it came to pass that, without any real friendly sympathy between them, Rosy had her cousin's confidence, and heard and saw more of her at this trying period of her life than anyone else.

I come now to the narration of an event which took the world by surprise. A few people who liked to be considered very shrewd and clever, professed to have seen signs of it long before; but I confess that, with all my interest in those concerned, I had seen none.

"It is a fact, then, that Barrington is going to marry the Lady Augusta Leigh?" was Squire Sylvester's startling interrogatory one day when we met him on the road to Beechcroft. He saw that I was struck dumb—as for my dear Arthur nothing ever did astonish him. "They were full of the news at the Club House in Gladestone—I have just come out of Gladestone. And you have not heard it? Has not his daughter been told?"

"I saw her less than an hour ago with Rosy Bethell, and I am sure that neither had heard a syllable of such a thing then. It cannot be true—it *cannot* be true!"

"The likeliest thing in the world! Barrington and Lady Augusta were always capital friends; and since the new duchess has deposed her ladyship, she may well be glad to accept a lesser sovereignty. How will Felicia like being superseded?"

Like it! she would not tolerate it!—We drove on to Beechcroft. Mr. Cartwright and Helen were both in, and I began straightway to out-pour to Helen. She took the intelligence quite calmly, and then Mr. Cartwright remembered that he had heard it the previous day, and had forgotten to tell her—of so light importance did it appear to them!

We really are of very small consequence to anybody whose personal interests are not involved with ours! "Every man's soul is alone," and every man's and woman's fate is isolated!—Arthur and I had driven out to make a round of calls, and we accomplished our object, meeting everywhere the same story, told and re-told with every variety of comment and speculation; and then dismissed for some other theme of local interest. The undisguised opinion of the majority was that the marriage of Mr. Barrington and Lady Augusta would be a very good thing. Lady Augusta was a woman of spirit, gay and sociable; she would revive the hospitalities of the Manor, which had been so spasmodic of late years, and the whole neighbourhood would be a gainer by it. Only Mrs. Claylands expressed anxiety for Felicia; everybody else assumed, as a matter of course, that she would give place to her father's wife, that she ought to do so, and that whether she liked it or not was of no moment except to herself. In obliterating herself for her father once, Felicia seemed, in the popular judgment, to have forfeited any right of self-assertion for the future; and Ringwood had been so diligent to knead its calumnies into the popular belief, that many persons who did not know her, or who knew her but slightly, had formed a fantastic caricature of her as a very poor creature indeed, and very easily to be set aside.

I returned home from my visits in the most annoyed frame of mind possible, but determined to sleep on what I had heard before seeing Felicia. Intimately as I knew her, I could form no conjecture of how she would act in this new and unforeseen emergency;—probably the sentiments of other people had confused my own ideas.

The next morning, not ten minutes after post-time, Rosy Bethell rushed across to the Rectory, fussy, excited, a-grin. "Oh! what do you think, Mrs. Gower?" cried she, breathless: "what *do* you think? *Uncle Barrington is going to be married!* Felicia has had a letter from her papa and Lady Augusta to tell her that they are *going to be married!* When she had read it, she sprang up from the breakfast-table in such a rage, and holding it up with both her hands, tore it in two—*so:*" (imitating the violent action of tearing something held on a level with her head). "I declare I am quite frightened of her! will you come and try to pacify her? She has locked herself in the boudoir; and you would never guess what she vowed in her fury—'I'll marry the first man that asks me!' that she did! so here is Captain Gresham's opportunity, if he likes to come forward again. Did you ever hear such a complication out of a novel? I wonder what papa will say—if he knows yet. I must positively go over to Ringwood, and tell him."

"Don't tell everything you hear and see, Rosy—that is not loyal to Felicia, living under the same roof with her," said I, in a warning way; for I had a terror of Rosy's ridiculous chatter.

"No, I won't—if I *did*, what *would* people think?" rejoined she, with a meaning smile.

I did not pick up the glove. It had dawned on me lately that Rosy enjoyed a dispute about her Cousin Felicia, and since the discovery I had been cautious to decline her challenges; for I found she repeated abroad what she said to me, without repeating my answers; and, of course, the effect was that she invariably appeared to have had the best of the argument. Nor did I accede to her proposal to intrude upon Felicia with premature attempts at pacification. She would be better alone for a while, to digest what I now recognized as the cruellest mortification that she could have been called upon to suffer. Since her return from London, after the settlement of her father's affairs, she had talked of him pleasantly, and had given all of us who cared to listen to understand that henceforward she had no prospects for herself apart from him, and that her life was to be wholly devoted to his service. I believe, poor girl, she dreamed sometimes of making a very fine thing of it, and was almost deluded into admiring her self-renunciation. And already, before the lapse of a month, she was apprized that her sacrifices must be their own reward—that, so far as her father was concerned, they were literally wasted and thrown away. It was easy to put myself in her place, and to realize the passionate tumult of anger, disappoïntment, and indignation that must have arisen in her bosom as she read the letter that brought the tidings.

When I read it, it put *me* in a rage; and yet it did no more than bear out what I had predicted from the beginning. It was the coolest document! Not one plea, not one apology, did

Mr. Barrington offer; but frankly assumed that his lady-wife would be as welcome at the Manor as himself; that Felicia would be glad and grateful for her coming, and would gracefully resign to Lady Augusta the place and precedence which her rank, and her position as his wife, entitled her to.

And there was very little room to doubt, judging from foregone events, that Felicia would actually fulfil her expectations.

She brought the letter to me herself.

"You have heard the news, but read it," she said, and watched me to observe its effect.

There was nothing, I told her, to be done but to submit with a grace, whatever she thought or felt. Lady Augusta's enclosure was kind in feeling, but she had a very high notion of what her rights at the Manor would be—*her* rights in what was absolutely Felicia's house. Oh! how I wished my darling could marry to her heart's content, and defeat them all!

If Felicia's fury had been as hot and uncontrolled at first, as Rosy described it, it had sunk now into a cold, concentrated resolve not to fret herself for what she could not hinder, but to go henceforth her own way, and let her father go his, with the friends of his choice. She did not hark back upon the old grievance for his sake—she had become timidly reserved about that, it was not difficult to discern why; nor did she repeat to me the threat which Rosy had quoted as the first utterance of her wrath. If she had not forgotten, she was probably ashamed of it. I had turned very cautious of what I said to her with regard to the future. Helen had told me that she did not find Captain Gresham improved either in feeling or principle since he went away, and she blamed Felicia for his deterioration—no one else, that I could discover, shared my sister's views. People, in general, liked him more than ever. *Me* he had not come near—I could excuse his reluctance to see Stone leigh again, and did not wonder at it.

"In the long run Felicia's faithlessness has done him harm," Helen said. "It might not appear at first, perhaps, when his heart was sore and tender; but since the wound has healed, he is hardened—he speaks of himself as having succumbed to the common lot, and laughs at the pain which was real enough while it lasted. He reminds me occasionally of Mr. Ralph Barrington in the style he talks of women—women are charming playthings, very pretty toys for idle hours; but the man is a fool who puts himself in their power, when he can help it."

I asked if she thought he had any lingering sentiments for his lost love.

She was sure he had, his distrust of himself was so evident. He confessed to an unwillingness to meet her lest his fair memory of her should be sullied, or the flame of his betrayed passion scorch him again. He was somewhat proud and resentful; and Helen expressed a strong opinion that, whatever his regrets, he had neither the intention nor the desire to re-knit their broken bonds. I, knowing this, and knowing that a quite contrary hope haunted Felicia's mind, had to keep a strict watch upon my lips when I was with her.

Mr. Barrington arrived at the Manor about ten days after the news of his engagement was spread;

and almost immediately afterwards, he and Felicia paid a visit to the Castle. Lady Augusta's marriage was sufficiently prudent to give the duke satisfaction. We heard that it was to be celebrated at Lowndes, shortly after Christmas, and that the settlements were in course of preparation already. Mr. Tom Bethell said of Mr. Barrington, that there was no fool like an old fool; but added, that it was impossible he could be adverse to a match which would assure to his unfortunate niece a judicious guardian—Lady Augusta was a woman of sense, and if any one *could*, she would keep Felicia from making a show of herself.

I did not know what he meant, nor did I inquire. He was in a complacent humour. Mr. Barrington's marriage contravened no expectations of his, and he did not anticipate the disaster to his secret hopes which was to issue from it. Neither certainly did I, notwithstanding Felicia's rash vow, which Rosy had reported to me—and not to me only as I discovered by-and-by.

CHAPTER VII.

THE DEATH OF HOPE.

"CAPTAIN GRESHAM has taken himself off out of harm's way—he is gone for a prolonged tour on the continent with his sister!" This announcement came from Rosy Bethell with a most triumphant giggle. "Yes, he has fairly run away from temptation! I wish you could have been witness to a little scene in our drawing-room at home, not a week ago, Mrs. Gower; it would have amused you—have interested you, that is."

I did not answer a word; the information affected me profoundly. Rosy disposed herself to tell her story: she had ridden from Ringwood on purpose. I will give it as nearly as possible in her own manner. Nothing Rosy delighted in, nothing she delights in still, so much as a long story to tell!

"You know Captain Gresham likes mamma, and he has been as often to see us at Ringwood as he has been anywhere since he came from India, though papa and he are not particular friends. Well, you must understand that I had related to mamma at the time, the ridiculous farce Felicia enacted when she read Uncle Barrington's letter about his marriage, that is to be, with Lady Augusta; and it seems that Bobby, that little pitcher with long ears, was there, and heard every word—who would have suspected Bobby of listening to anything? Mamma's easy good-nature is notorious; everybody would be happy if she had the making of their fates, and I know she stood up to papa for Felicia and her Prince Charming when they were so desperately in love—she is very romantic, poor mamma! After they had talked (Captain Gresham and mamma, I mean) over the coming alliance between the Castle and the Manor, there was a word or two said of the dowager's silly scheme for marrying Felicia to the Marquis, and

Captain Gresham got fidgety—one could see that the very name of her was a thorn! But mamma did not notice, and went on—praised her, pitied her, said her fate was tragical; she was a lovely creature, the most unselfish, generous, kindly creature—and for her part, *she* (mamma) did not believe that Felicia's mind had ever been any more unhinged than sorrow might unhinge the mind of any of us. Felicia's adoption of Bobby has quite won mamma's heart, you must know! Captain Gresham, while she talked, went marching up and down the room with such a face! I hardly liked to look at him—one does not like to see a great, strong man so moved—it is far worse than one of us. Talk of his having forgotten Felicia, of his not caring for her now!—He has no more forgotten her than she has forgotten him; he is as mad for her as ever, and if they once met, it would be all over with his stern resolves! What a *strange* thing love is, Mrs. Gower!—I cannot understand it one bit—not as it affects those two. Of course, I love people myself; I hope I love everybody—even my enemies, if I have any——"

Rosy paused to take breath in her perplexity, and I said, for I was growing sick with pity: "When are you coming to Bobby's part in the story? Bobby ought to be Felicia's leal friend and servitor."

"So he is. It was an unlucky speech of mine brought *him* to the fore—my saying that I expected poor, dear Felicia would lead a happy retired life enough amongst us, when she had Lady Augusta to guide her, and it was very unlikely she would marry in her sad circumstances—for I wanted him to go away a little comforted—when that terrible Bobby shouts: 'Oh! Rosy, how *can* you tell such a *story*, when Cousin Felicia cried out that she should marry the first man who asks her?'—Captain Gresham stood stock-still for a minute, glaring at poor Bobby as if he could have eaten him; and then he turned short round to mamma, and said he must be off—he had stayed an unconscionable time—had made her quite a visitation. And he was off with a vengeance! for the next day we heard that he had gone to Dover, and we have heard since that

Mrs. Willis has joined him there, and they are to spend the winter in Italy."

I had learnt from my sister Helen already that such a journey was projected at Fairfield, for the planning of which guide-books had been borrowed from Mr. Cartwright, and much general information sought, such as only those who have gone over the ground can supply, so that Captain Gresham's flight was not so sudden and undesigned as Rosy imagined.

She proceeded to point the moral of the occasion: "Now, I *respect* a man like Captain Gresham—he has the courage so few men possess. He loves Felicia awfully, and even *you* don't pity her more; but he knows what she has gone through, and that he ought not to marry her—for no one ought to marry who lies under the risk of insanity. Papa says so, and it is quite my idea too. And then, whatever her plea, she did not behave well to him in throwing him over before: *I* consider she was right, but *he* may be excused if he thinks differently. The wonder is that he has not become perfectly careless about her——."

"If the fear of her sanity is Captain Gresham's only reason for putting half a continent between himself and Felicia, he might easily have informed himself of the truth—but it is *not*. He has not forgiven her weakness two years ago," said I.

"It is hardly to be expected that he should have forgiven it—is it now, Mrs. Gower?" Rosy urged. "A man of spirit is not to be whistled on and off at a girl's pleasure—papa says so. Captain Gresham bore some harsh imputations when he was engaged to Felicia—we hear no more of them *now*, because he has come into possession of Fairfield; but he was horribly poor *then*, and his mother looked a woman who might live to be a hundred! Then those old uncles who left him their money—he had no expectations from them—or if he had, he kept them to himself—and how was anybody to know? He was considered nothing of a match when we called him Prince Charming:—but at this day, I suppose there is not a more eligible match in the county. So why should he take up again with poor Felicia, at second-hand, as one may say? You have been indulging hopes that he *might;* and now you see his practical commentary on such vain expectations. 'Best safety lies in fear,' and he has gone where he will be clear of the peril of falling under her fascination once more, a weakness of which such a proud man would bitterly repent."

Perhaps Rosy interpreted Captain Gresham justly. For my part I thought then, and think still, that it would have been better wisdom to let the love which had survived so much, overrule both his pride and his prudence.

We were now in September—far advanced in September, but there were still beautiful warm days, when a walk on the hills was pleasant as summer. Felicia invited me often to walk with her of an afternoon, and drifting Jack and Lizzie before us, we had many a long range over the green fields and brown stubble. Felicia's fancy was to be upon the heights, when we could see afar off. The day following Rosy's visit to me, we had one of these walks, and Felicia gave me to understand that what Rosy had told me, she had heard before. Her manner was very subdued, her voice low, and her conversation intermittent. That was the only reference she made to Captain Gresham—her intimation that she knew he had gone abroad. When she spoke again, it was of the scenery before our eyes, of the declining season, of little incidents in the village, or of the children, who reckoned it a most prodigious honour to be taken out by mamma and Cousin Felicia instead of by nurse.

We returned through the bank, that hillside plantation at the back of the Manor, whence we could overlook the pleasant country and the windings of the river. The children were fond of this little wood; it was all safe, no traps or ugly ditches to fall into, but fenced and kept like a garden. Secure from harm, they ran hither and thither at their own wild will, while Felicia and I sought a sheltered seat to rest; for she was tired, and yet it was delightful out-of-doors.

The difficulty of making conversation on things indifferent who does not know! Felicia and I never attempted it. We knew each other well enough to be silent when we had nothing to say, or when our minds were heavy with thoughts best left unspoken, as they were now. The avenue of young limes that Felicia had planted three years ago, for love of the limes at Hampton Court, were shedding their yellow leaves already, but the oak-copses were deep green still. The afternoon was very hushed; not a breeze, not a twig stirred, and the pale amber sky was without a cloud. At intervals came the ring of a shot beyond the shoulder of the hill, where Mr. Barrington or the keeper was making war upon the partridges; and then the peculiar note of the cowherd calling the cattle up from the ings at milking-time.

"Very pastoral and very monotonous, Clare," remarked Felicia as the mild patient beasts came up from the river, and trooped towards the gate.

"It is enough for me; I never tire of country sights and sounds," said I. "Here our lot is cast, and here I am content to live and die. It would grieve more than it would please me, if Arthur were made a canon or precentor, or anything else dignified, that would oblige us to go and vegetate in a dull cathedral close."

"You have no ambition, Clare."

"I have happiness, and that is better."

"What is a woman to do who has neither? To let life stagnate?"

There was no visitor staying at the Manor just now. Mr. Barrington and his daughter had the house to themselves, and Felicia was glad of it. "We shall never be alone again, perhaps," was her reflection; but doubtless some of the many hours of the day went with leaden feet. Hope and expectation are wings on which time flies—now time for her had folded its wings, and walked wearily on the earth.

Any incident to break the level dulness was welcome. We heard the voices of persons approaching, and Felicia rose to look who was at hand.

"It is George Sylvester, with papa—good old George," said she, and went forward to meet them.

George had his gun and dogs too, and bore a jovial, well-tanned visage. Felicia was smiling as she turned back with them, and they all sat a little while, where we two had been sitting alone before. George, it seemed, had come to Bylands for a week's sport—the sport in Gladeshire was better than in Essex, but he meant to remedy that by strict preserving. He had been in Scotland for the moor-game — sport was the breath of his nostrils—without it, life was naught—that was George's philosophy. He throve well in spite of his love deferred and disappointed, but in a bad hunting-country he should pine away and die—so he cheerfully assured us all with a charming absence of sentimentality. Then he complimented Felicia on her improved appearance of health, and talked of his sister Jenny's wedding. Jenny was marrying a born Nimrod, after his own and Squire Sylvester's heart, and George was greatly gratified by her choice.

"A good, sensible girl Jenny is, no nonsense about her; Warren is a good, sensible fellow, too, and one is as lucky as the other," was his style of commendation; and then he looked at Felicia as much as to say: "Why cannot you and I be sensible too?"

Felicia turned away with a heightened colour in her face, and Mr. Barrington jumped up, and preceded us to the house.

Lady Augusta Leigh arrived at the Manor while George Sylvester was at Bylands. Her ladyship was in the disposition to make Felicia happy if she could; and as it was a settled arrangement that the Manor should be her residence with Mr. Barrington after their marriage, it is not impossible but that she had an eye to her own comfort in seeking to provide his daughter with another home before that event took place.

"Felicia is not to wear the willow all her life," was Lady Augusta's expression in talking over her plans with me. "Tom Bethell has played a clever game against very poor antagonists, but he shows his hand now, and shall not win it—It would suit his book that she should not marry—*not marry! ridiculous!* George Sylvester will do for her very well—they are such a perfect contrast. From this moment I declare myself George's advocate! It was very short-sighted, and a great pity to make her give up Captain Gresham—Fairfield would have been just a nice distance off—but that is over, and I don't think she can do better than take George. George is very fond of her, and always was. I have had some conversation with him, and he confesses that she is the only woman that he ever cared for."

I rejoined that Felicia's marriage with George Sylvester might be an event of the future, but that to force it on now was most undesirable.

"Why so? I have heard that hearts are best caught at the rebound," said Lady Augusta.

"The rebound is spent for Felicia, I'm afraid."

"Poor child, she has been cruelly ill-used! I should not have given Tom Bethell credit for so much craft as he has shown. His manœuvring has been masterly—but it shall have a check! I tell Mr. Barrington that, but for his ineradicable indolence, Felicia might have been joyfully married, the Yorkshire property saved, and he as quietly liberated from his embarrassments as he was. If I had known two years ago what I know now, I would have made him defy Tom Bethell, and brave the worst he could do. It would not have been so *very* bad! many and many a man has his private debts and losses, who grins and bears them, without putting his children's happiness in pawn. There must be a strain of this fatal easiness in Felicia, or when so much was required of her, she would have made her bargain."

"It was the peril to her father's life broke down her will," I pleaded.

"So they say. So she tells me herself—and I tell her again, that he should have *died* for me, before *I* would have done it!"

"And to *that*, what does she answer?"

"That she is glad she did; for if he had died, she should never have forgiven herself, and remorse of conscience is worse to bear than many miseries. Thus it is that the cowardice of the weak makes opportunities for the wicked. Thank God, my conscience is not so craven!"

Lady Augusta was an admirable daughter herself, and had been everything to her father in the interval between his two marriages. She had the credit of bringing about the last, and was said to have wished to promote it some years before, when the career of her only brother promised no long continuance. She could therefore afford to say that Felicia had overstepped the claims of filial duty in resigning her lover; and mutual friends felt that it would, perhaps, have been happier for the young lady of the Manor if her father had taken earlier, such a reasonable wife as he had now chosen.

But there is nothing so unprofitable as discussing the *might-have-beens!*

Common people exercise a certain delicacy and reserve in settling matrimonial engagements, but Lady Augusta went about her business of bringing George and Felicia to a good understanding as openly as if the transaction were a royal marriage. The idea was not new to anybody. The old story of Mrs. Barrington's having expressed a desire for their union on her death-bed was revived. That George was eager for it, he let the world know, and every member of his family supported him loyally. Lady Augusta prolonged her visit at the Manor, and George prolonged his at Bylands, and the intercourse between the two houses was very brisk. From what I saw of Felicia, I thought her apathetic, and felt a confidence that she would not be prevailed on to change her condition at present. But Lady Augusta had her ear, life hung on her hands wearily, and all hope of bettering it seemed dead—unless by violent means, such as this throwing herself into an entirely new circle of duties, in a strange place, and amongst unknown neighbours. I thought it a most perilous expedient—others advised it as the one thing essential to restore her to society—Helen and Mrs. Claylands quite seconded Lady Augusta.

Mr. Barrington, I believe, maintained a perfect neutrality, and trusted the guidance of his daughter's affairs to his future wife with implicit reliance on her tact in bringing them to a successful issue. He was pleased with the way in which Felicia had resigned herself to his approaching marriage, and with the friendliness she exhibited towards Lady Augusta. Not so the dowager. She was angry with Mr. Barrington for taking a second wife, and angry with Felicia for acquiescing in the alliance which would thrust her from her place of honour. The contemplated union of Felicia and George was laid before her. She looked surprised, trembled, hesitated, *remembered*, perhaps; and then she said George was an honest gentleman, farmer-like, and unpolished, but he would be good to his wife, and it might be the best match Felicia would have the opportunity of making *now*—it would be better that she should marry George, than not marry at all—and there was a long attachment on his side. And then the senile tears of weakness overflowed her eyes.

Mr. Tom Bethell was admitted behind the scenes early in this new act of Felicia's tragedy. I can scarcely forbear a smile even at this distance of time, when I recall how he was affected by it. First, amazement shook him to his centre; amazement that George Sylvester who, with his excellent character and fine estate in Essex, might have his pick and choice of wives, should condescend to Felicia Barrington, who had scorned him for years, and only accepted him now because she was scorned in her turn, and could not school her proud temper to live at home under a step-mother. Then disgust, or what he called disgust, at Felicia herself, whose extravagant behaviour had seemed a pledge that she would live and die for her love, taking *literally* the earliest chance of consolation that was offered to her! Then rage, sincerest of his sentiments, rage at the fine vanishing-point to which his dreams of Stoneleigh were reduced.—In this last paroxysm, he resigned his volunteer stewardship over the Manor, and Judd was made master in his room—not a very discreet appointment, but Judd was on the spot, he knew the property, and, as Mr. Barrington remarked, it saved trouble.

I believe that indolence, which is always saving itself trouble, is the root of half the mischief in the world!

CHAPTER VIII.

FELICIA SEEKS A REFUGE.

"It appears," said Felicia, "that no one is to suffer but myself. They have found their remedy —why should not I seek mine too? Like the poor body who married auld Robin Grey, I shall try my best a good wife to be."

"If that poor body had been only a little more patient, she might have had her Jamie," rejoined I.

The debateable question we were upon was whether Felicia should accept the formal proposal of George Sylvester, and marry him out of hand —that is, as fast as lawyers and milliners could transact their part in the business. I was very, *very* loth to hear a word of it, but Felicia insisted on my attention—my advice she did not ask, or that would soon have been given.

I believed that in marrying George *now* she would do foolishly—do madly, and no scruple prevented my telling her so. I pleaded hard with her to spare herself; pleaded for a year's delay—a year and a day was the time of the old song which would have saved his bride to Jamie—and *then*, if no place of repentance and reconciliation had been found for her and her once true lover, I promised not to urge any further probation, but to let her do what seemed to her best.

"If you had *seen* each other I would shut my lips, but you have not even *seen* each other," I insisted.

"It was not I who went out of the way, Clare. Would you have me sue to him for pardon? God knows that I am humbled, but I cannot put myself under his feet," replied Felicia, and covered her face with her hands.

"You still love one another," said I—for had not Rosy Bethell betrayed him to me as possessed by Felicia's image? and such love, if it gets the chance, will bear down many restraints. He might be proud, resentful; he might believe the false calumnies set afloat by Ringwood, and at one sight of her dear face, all the anger, malice, and evil-speaking might vanish from his remembrance, and leave only the ancient kindness. To whatever I advanced, she listened with a dreary, listless air, and bade me not indulge my credulous fancy, but consider what Captain Gresham had actually done.

This was natural, excusable; but she vext me by refusing to see anything wrong in marrying George Sylvester, though I declared that it was a shame to think of it, with her heart full of regret for another man; and that George must be very mean-spirited to take his wife on such terms. Her reply was not very satisfactory.

"Poor George, so *he* is content, what matters? He is the only person who really loves me—*you* don't, Clare, or you would not be so hard. I crave for rest. When I am married, I shall know that my life is irrevocably fixed. I shall have found a refuge, at least, if not a perfect home."

"A *refuge!* A place of torment, you mean?

If you were destitute of heart and conscience, it might be a refuge—"

"I don't feel any more that I have a heart—they have killed it amongst them."

"No, it is only benumbed with racking. You will find it alive, and keen enough to suffer again by and by."

"What should make me suffer any more? Not George—I can trust him to be both tender and patient with me—and that is all I ask. I wish the deed were done, and I anywhere but here! Everything renews my misery! I expected to find you ready to administer the common-places of philosophy, and glad to encourage me in this reasonable conclusion to my romance."

The worst of all was when Felicia mocked at herself! "If you marry George Sylvester before this year is out, I will not come to your wedding," cried I with angry decision.

"You don't mean that, Clare?" pleaded Felicia, softening again. "You will never forsake me when I have such need of you? I shall want your help and counsel in so many ways."

"Then you *may* want them; for neither hand nor voice will I lend to the furtherance of this new sacrifice of yourself until you have had time and leisure, for second thoughts. That is my last word on the matter, and tears shall not move me!"

"Invincible little woman, perhaps, kisses will," and she made a feint of kissing me; but I pushed her off, and she went away laughing at my display of energy. She did not believe that I should keep my word, but I was never more in earnest

Before we had this conversation Felicia's mind was positively made up. When neighbours met, almost the first words spoken were:—"Well, we hear that George Sylvester is to marry Miss Barrington — she does not like the notion of giving place to Lady Augusta, we understand. And when is the marriage to take place? before her father's, of course."

Yes, it was to precede Mr. Barrington's. A very little while after I had uttered my threat of absence from her wedding, Felicia herself told me that it was to be in Christmas week—and then she tried to melt my obdurate resolve by all the wiles at her command.

"Consider what you do, Clare," she urged with a sweet gravity very hard to resist. "On my wedding-day ends my life and reign at the Manor. We shall no more run to and fro to each other as we have done. All the cottagers will come on Christmas Eve, and I shall never distribute my Christmas gifts to them again—that will be Lady Augusta's duty, and I shall have to find poor folks to bless me amongst a strange people. For the last time, Clare, will you come and see me married? Your absence will be my only sorrow if you don't, and it will grieve me mightily."

I cannot tell now what gave me strength and courage to stick to my determination, but I did stick to it. She said that she had not believed I could be so unkind, and George would take it very much amiss.

"You don't fear that I shall put him to shame on his wedding-day, by looking like a ghost, and weeping like a cloud, do you?" she went on. I disdained any such fear. "I promise you that

I shall be every inch the happy bride! Nobody shall pity George for my tears. I have done with tears! It will be a splendid occasion, with half the county for witnesses—George likes a hospitable magnificence, and the Manor will put forth all its strength to gratify him. And you won't come, Clare?"

"You will have witnesses enough without me. If you don't weep for yourself, I might weep for you—I'll stop at home, and pray instead—prayers will serve you better."

"Prayers? I won't refuse them—it is not many I say now on my own account. I cannot go deliberately against my conscience, and kneel down in the face of God, and ask Him to help me."

"Then you *are* going against your conscience in this marriage, Felicia?"

She assented with a nod, and the next moment retracted, trying to extenuate or explain. In one sense, she had gone against her conscience in each material crisis of her life; her sense of right and wrong had fallen into confusion, and she was letting those guide her who professed to be clear in their judgment, and able to direct her for the best. I invited her to say why she excluded me from the list of her counsellors. She replied because I was only another *self.*

"I acknowledge my responsibility, however," she added. "I blame no one for what has befallen me in the past, for what I am about to venture on, or for what may come of it. If you shrink from the chance of my reproaching you some day, should you give me the light of your countenance at my wedding, I pledge myself that never will I reproach you or any other person—take my word, Clare; relent, and lift a load off my mind."

I shook my head.

"Then we are not to talk of it? Grannie is too old to consult—she forgets things. Ringwood is so far off—Lady Augusta is kind, but I cannot be confidential with *her*. You are my one intimate, married friend; mamma bespoke you for me; and just at this pass, you set your face against me, and will take no interest in my most vital concerns."

I looked up at her; she was smiling rosily as if she believed that yield I must. I was on the brink of it, but that smile hardened me again, and then she professed to see that my obstinacy was unconquerable.

"So be it, then. I will advise with Janet and Carr, and entrust the choice of my wedding garments to Madame Elise."

This was not the last argument by many that we had on the same theme, but the end of it never varied. My purpose was fixed. I would not go to Felicia's wedding with George Sylvester; and the nearer the event drew on, the less my heart, judgment and conscience rebuked me for what had, at first, looked like an obstinate, unkind piece of overstrained virtue.

I never, from the moment the marriage was once publicly announced, indulged one expectation that it would be broken off. Too many persons were interested in its accomplishment. Mr. Barrington entered into the business with spirit. He was glad, he said, to see his dear Felicy so happy once more, blooming like a rose, gay, active, musical as a bird—his paternal fondness exaggerated the gaiety, but let that pass; she was perpetually in movement, and seemed to be gay. Then he was glad also that he and Lady Augusta were to hold undivided possession of Stoneleigh. It was put in this light, and even Mr. Tom Bethell could not find a reason against it—One country-house was enough for the young married people to maintain in liberal style: George Sylvester was bound to live for so many months in the year on his Essex property until he had held it for ten; his house there was a rival for Felicia's birthplace, in antiquity and beauty, and whatever her preference might have been under other circumstances she desired to submit it entirely to his wishes now: It would be much more profitable and pleasant for Stoneleigh to have a resident squire and lady, all agreed, than to be deserted: A village must suffer by an absentee proprietor, and Mr. Barrington and Lady Augusta were made heartily welcome to live there, for the performance of Felicia's functions. But that the young lady of the Manor was going away, to make her home amongst strangers, was a sad drawback from her marriage in the eyes of the villagers, to whom she was very dear. As for me, I averted my thoughts from it whenever I could—it seemed to me that Stoneleigh would be no more like itself when she was gone.

Squire Sylvester was as jubilant as anybody over the coming event. It never entered his honest mind that Felicia was not heart and soul for George now as she had been once for Captain Gresham. He was extremely proud of her, and spoke as if they two had been born and brought up for each other, and no love-episode had intervened. George himself was jubilant and proud too, and was endeavouring to be more of the carpet-knight and less of the rude esquire—yet, now and then, a transient cloud obscured his joy, a doubt, a suspicion, a dread. It could not be otherwise, unless he had been more vain and foolish than is possible to a true heart—for he, at least, was not ignorant of what Felicia had felt and suffered for another lover before him.—How had she put his haunting memory aside? she made me wonder sometimes, when she talked of

London, of the fortunate proximity of Essex to town, and of the pleasures of the season, as if they bounded her desires! George Sylvester, I knew, had not much taste for them, but they entered largely into her plans of life. I thought to myself when I thus heard her discourse: "She will soon become a thorough woman of the world, and we shall lose her quite!"

"Let us hope it will turn out all for the best," was the easy philosophy of Felicia's friends in general. Her present engagement carried many minds back to her previous one—to the Peace Celebration, to the Hunt Ball at Gladestone, when Captain Gresham was her hero—but what more frequent, as they judiciously observed, than for young people to have a violent love-fit, to see it brought to a violent end, and to find their future peace and contentment in a moderate and homely affection? It was the common lot, if I would believe their testimony—or, if I would look round amongst the families of my neighbours, I could verify the assertion for myself.

But this was precisely what I denied. For one

woman whom I saw capable of the intense passion of Felicia, there were a score of the ruminative, cow-like temperament of Rosy Bethell, ready to like anybody who liked them, whose love, before marriage, never exceeded a gentle preference, or blinded them to the material advantages of a suitor:—safer and better for the world and for society, I grant; more comfortable and pleasant in every way; but a dire mistake it is, when the finer, exceptional natures, torn with anguish, let themselves be driven by that narrow rule. Felicia would have done more wisely to remain free, if ever so melancholy and lonely, than to put herself under the bonds which were elastic enough for them—to remain free, at least, until the cure of her original wound was more complete. She was young, and youth has vast recuperative powers, but her own impatience, and the impatience of some who considered their own pleasure in the matter rather than her good, robbed her of her last chance of permanent healing. I told her once and again that she would sorrow to the longest day she had to live for what she was now bent on doing; but it was like talking to the wind! She imagined she saw escape into a new world where old griefs would not follow her, and she was in haste to get away, and shut a door upon the past. As if she could! as if she *could!*

Whether her pride was involved in all this? Doubtless, to some extent, it was. That bitter farewell to Captain Gresham before he went to India, was meant to be final. And yet, as events had turned, it need not have been final—delay would have served as well as division—better than division. Felicia had feared too much, and had lost all. She was ever in extremes—this sudden acceptance of George Sylvester—what was *that* but an extreme, a desperate, irrevocable step? I have reason to know that long after his departure, Captain Gresham did not relinquish his idea of reclaiming Felicia; but letters from home carried to his ears every injurious story propagated at Ringwood, and especially the false rumour that her mind had given way under her poignant distress. There was nothing incredible in this, and I impute no blame to him that he believed it, or that it altered his intentions towards her: that it did not kill his ardent passion was proved but too sadly in the sequel. What I do say is that with love, warm and sensitive in his heart still, he should have been kinder to himself and her, that he should have diligently sought out the truth, and have had courage to see her face once more, before seeking safety from the temptation of his noblest feelings in a cautious flight.

When he returned to England there were more voices to asseverate the truth of the lies that had been written to him than to deny them; and it is *possible* that he *did* congratulate himself on his freedom,—*possible*, but *I* do not credit it. Still it was reported of him, and brought to Felicia's knowledge by her Cousin Rosy, that indefatigable tattler, who said she had it from Miss Reed. And *that* was the nail clinched Felicia's mad resolution. She was too credulous by far. Of some men it might have been safely predicated that they would say such a thing, but not of

Captain Gresham. His devotion, his chivalry had a defect, or he would have given his life for her, as she had almost given hers for him—but that he ever uttered one cynical or unkind word against her, no power on earth shall make me believe! Our friendship has been close enough in recent years, and I know that Felicia lives in his remembrance always with a profound and passionate regret.

CHAPTER IX.

ANOTHER CHRISTMAS EVE.

All the principal guests who were to be in the house for the wedding were there on Christmas Eve, and Lady Augusta, looking extraordinarily handsome and happy, took a prominent part in the distribution of the bounties over which Felicia presided. Next year she would preside herself, and Felicia would have been transported to another sphere of charity.

I was in the gallery on this occasion, watching the scene without participating in it. The afternoon was overcast and gloomy, but the blaze of the yule logs contended successfully against the winter clouds, and in the hall there was no lack of light, warmth and good cheer. The evergreen decorations had been done with unusual care to last the week over, and a peculiar interest was stirring amongst the people, though, whether to seem more joyful or a little sad was clearly a puzzle to many.

Felicia looked grand and beautiful, but why had she dressed herself in *black* velvet? Because it was warm? It was one of the new dresses for her wedding, very rich and elegant, but she had others as warm, and more suitable—Grandmother Burt asked what she had put on mourning for, and Arthur remarked that black velvet reminded him of a pall. However, it was her whim, and her appearance was very distinguished.

Mr. Barrington had a pleasant word for everybody, and a most assiduous kindness for his daughter. He was in excellent humour: a complete contrast to poor Mr. Tom Bethell, who sat in a corner of the gallery behind his younger children, looking a picture of acrid, wrinkled disgust. He was not to say an *old* man yet, but he was beginning to show very obviously that he was a long way from young. Miss Reed, who was present also, in the character of children's governess, had a bitter countenance too, and if they were reminded of their last Christmas Eve in that house, and of the humiliation which then overtook them, they had good cause for dark looks.

Janet had brought me a message from Felicia to go to the boudoir when the distribution was over, and thither I adjourned, and waited for her coming. She came at length, accompanied by a troop of cousins, Amy, Dulcy, Mab, a little sister of George Sylvester's, and two or three girls beside, all full of mirth and laughter.

"We are to see the wedding things! we are to see the wedding things!" cried Mab, and twirled round on her toes, clapping her hands above her head, and executing a series of capers, expressive of the liveliest delight. All the young faces were glowing with pleasure, all the young eyes shone round and bright with curiosity and expectation—such a charm and mystery is there about "wedding things!"

"Now, young ladies, you must not *crush*," I heard Janet say with respectful decision, as they crowded out of the boudoir into the bed-room adjoining. Then what a noise they made, what a tumult of admiration and wonder at the "beauties of dresses" they were privileged to behold.

Felicia stood on the hearth, hearing them, and smiling to herself, and presently, with a gleam of mischief in her eyes, she said: "I know, Clare, that you are dying to see them too:"—for it was a fact that I had not seen any of her gauds or splendours; I had not even inquired one word about them, but I was quite willing to see them if she wished it.

We moved to the doorway of the next room, where a profound hush had fallen suddenly. Mab had pleaded to try on the wedding-wreath and veil, and Janet, having wrapped her round first in a white sheet, to represent the dress, was adjusting the crown of orange and myrtle on her fair head. Mab had turned grave all at once, and so had the others, and the manœuvre was being executed with as much seriousness as if it were in earnest. Felicia and I held back, to observe the pretty pretence, ourselves unobserved; and then the veil was draped over the white sheet, and Mab paced solemnly to the cheval-glass, and contemplated herself with infinite satisfaction. We called her "little Mab," but she was a slender, rather tall figure, with a promise of most graceful dignity in her girlish, mimic airs.

As the fancy-bride looked in the mirror, I suppose she caught sight of our two faces peering in at the doorway, for she turned round blushing furiously, and crying out that she did not know Cousin Felicia was there.

"And what if I am?" said Felicia, and bestowed two kisses on the innocent roses of her cheeks, which emboldened Mab to express a hope that *he* would be nice—the *he* for whom she should some day wear a bridal crown and veil, *not in fun.*

"Perhaps you will never get fallen in love with," suggested Dulcy.

"*Oh!*" chorussed the witnesses, while Mab tossed her lovely little nose in the air with merry scorn at such a ridiculous notion—when everybody, from her papa downwards, was in love with her already! Dulcy rejoined that she was a conceited monkey, and there was imminent peril of tears, when happily a diversion was created by a summons for the Ringwood girls to go; their carriage was at the door, and their father waiting.

The dowager had left her own house for a week to stay at the Manor during the festivities which were to precede and follow the wedding; and Felicia and I had not been five minutes alone after the flight of the young people, when she came to the door of the boudoir, inquiring: "Is my Felicy here?"

"Yes, grannie, I am here, come in," cried my darling, and went forward, brought the old lady to the fireside, and with the tenderest affection, established her on her favourite couch.

The dowager was arrayed in pomp of velvet and Spanish point, but her withered face looked wan and troubled, and it was with very timid eyes, indeed, that she surveyed Felicia while she gave an account of Mab in her borrowed finery. From one thing to another they drifted into talking of the last wedding that had been at the Manor—the wedding of Felicia's parents, and the grandmamma had many little reminiscences of that event which it pleased her to recite. Felicia listened for some time attentively, but by-and-by, from her abstracted air, and gaze fixed on the embers, I perceived that she was far away in thought from those old-world stories. What pictures saw she in the fire? Dismal pictures, for her vision grew obscure with thick tears, and as the dowager prosed on, they fell like rain.

"Yes, your dear mamma was as happy a bride as ever the sun shone on; her mild persistence won the day—she had only me to contend with; I loved her, and was easily overborne. So she had her own will, and if it did not prove quite so pleasant as she fondly anticipated, yet she never acknowledged to regretting it—she did not regret it. And with all his faults poor Alfred, your papa, I mean, Felicia, was kind to her. It was hard on him, so gay and devoted to society as he was, to be encumbered with an invalid wife. Lucilla felt that, and bore very patiently with his long and frequent absences. But it was bad for him to have so much liberty, and bad for the property. I hope you will have your health, and will manage better with your Prince Charming."

The dowager seemed quite unconscious of this slip of the tongue, but Felicia kindled at it. dashed away her tears, and corrected her: "With George Sylvester, grannie, or George Sylvester-Constable, as we ought to call him."

"Ah, yes! with George. What was I dreaming about? My memory is not so clear as it was, and now and then I put one name for another. George Sylvester is a most excellent young man; I have a perfect confidence that he will do you justice. He has no fortune, but his family is honourable, and you have enough for both. Captain Gresham has left the country, I understand? You did not meet him anywhere in society before his departure?"

"No, grannie, we have not met for two years and over. He is travelling in Italy with his sister—Mrs. Willis."

"I am glad to know that. Two years is a long time to learn to forget. I hope he will keep out of your way on his return to England, when you are married, Felicy—the world is very cruel and malicious."

"I have learnt that lesson by heart already, grannie."

"And *you* are very impetuous, dear. It is wise to be on your guard—to be afraid of yourself."

"Why afraid? Do you think I shall find a traitor in my bosom? If I thought so I would not go to church with George the day after to-morrow. I feel firmly purposed to be dutiful, cheerful, and contented with him."

"And are you able to ask the blessing of God on your marriage, Felicy?" said the old lady, tremulously.

"*That* the clergyman does—does he not? I have not thought much of God and heavenly things of late, grannie—my life has fallen somehow out of harmony with them. But all the same, I trust God *will* bless us (if God meddles with our little joys and sorrows), and especially that he will never suffer me to be a disappointment to George—who is the very soul of honour, and most generous and good to me. He deserves all my love, and he has it."

"That is a right feeling, dear, and I am glad to hear you express it. Mrs. Gower is glad too, I know—we have differed in times past, but we shall agree as to that. But you must not forsake religion—without religion there is no happiness. Your dear mamma was a very good woman; Mrs. Gower knows that."

Felicia did not look to me for acquiescence at either appeal.

It was a relief when Janet brought in afternoon tea, and a message that the gentlemen were coming up in a few minutes to share it. It must be confessed that Felicia was learning her part admirably. Janet's message sent her to her mirror, from which she came back with countenance all composed. George had a right to look proud, to settle by her side as in his own place, to whisper his little confidential endearments, to glow in the light of her presence; for she welcomed him with a most cordial kindness. To a stranger they would have seemed a happy pair of lovers enough; and for a few minutes a qualm of regret troubled me concerning my vow not to look on at their wedding.

Mr. Barrington had expected to find Lady Augusta in the boudoir; she was not there, and he did not stay long. George had few subjects of conversation; his favourite subject was sport, and after a brief, often interrupted discourse of things in general, he proceeded to entertain his lady-love with the recital of yesterday's run with the fox-hounds, and grew animated, almost eloquent, before the poor beast of a fox was run to death.

Felicia seemed attentive and responsive. She had all the air of being interested until the narrative was brought to a triumphant conclusion, and George was gratified in the highest degree. I have a lively recollection of his honest rosy face and blue eyes turned to Felicia, as he rubbed his hands joyously, and asked if it was not "capital" —meaning the finis of his story.

"*Capital!*" echoed Felicia, and looked away towards the window smiling:—yet I doubt whether she could have given any account of what he had been telling her with such unction.

She had fallen into a habit of abstraction which grew upon her—fortunately George was not of a tenacious disposition. When he perceived that he wearied her, he was silent, or talked of something else. It was always a marvel to me why he should have set his mind on marrying her: they had no tastes in common,—nothing in common except the kindly familiarity of two young people, who have known and liked each other from childhood. However, there they were, within two days of their marriage, and Felicia was turning aside with a suppressed yawn from George's long hunting story.

I felt less reconciled to their union than ever!

CHAPTER X.

MARRIED IN HASTE.

The day was winterly, dark, without sun from morning till night.

It was a very splendid wedding, but I saw nothing of it. While it was going on I had the house to myself; for Arthur was one of the officiating clergymen, and children, nurse, servants, all must needs go to be witnesses of the fine spectacle in church. The clamour of the bells breaking out suddenly overhead, warned me when the ceremony was at an end, and presently Arthur came in home before going to the breakfast, and found me in my drawing-room alone, and nearly in the dark.

"Well, little stubborn wife, you have kept your

word, and are repenting of it, I don't doubt," was his first remark, and then he added: "But you need not have put the blinds down—the Rectory looks more as if there were a funeral than a wedding;" and he proceeded to draw them up, and to let in the light upon me, until he perceived that I had been crying.

"It was over now, and I might dry my tears." Arthur appealed to my common-sense whether what had been done that morning was not well done. But I could not acquiesce. "No," I said, "my instinctive feeling is as strong against it as ever; but since it is a fact accomplished, I am dumb."

I asked him how Felicia bore herself. He said that she was radiantly beautiful: rather pale at first, but before the ceremony was over, flushed and brilliant; and she had signed the book with as firm a hand as ever she had written her name in her life. George Sylvester, on the contrary, was nervous; but the person most of all agitated was the poor dowager, who almost fainted, and had to be taken out of church. Mr. Barrington was seriously light-hearted, and Mr. Tom Bethell was haggard as a death's head at a feast. The bridesmaids were eight, a bevy of beauties, and the friends and guests were a multitude:—so far Arthur's information. Minor details of the so-called "happy day," he left me to learn from Helen, from Rosy Bethell, or any other witness intimate enough to know my sentiments on the occasion.

The bells went on jingling and jangling, making anything but a joyous riot to my ears. The children came in, dined, went to the nursery to play, and still I wasted the hours in idle disquiet, expecting nothing, regretting nothing; afraid to stir out lest I should encounter my neighbours, to whom my absence from the wedding was explained by the politic fiction of an attack of influenza; and unable to settle to any useful task until the bridal pair were gone. I thought, when the wheels of their carriage were heard on the road, I would open the window, and wave Felicia a farewell; and for that moment I sat waiting and listening a full hour before it was likely to arrive.

I must have been sunk in a very deep reverie,—but, indeed, the bells drowned every other sound—when all at once I was aware of not being alone in the room, and, turning with a start, there I saw Felicia standing, all in blue silk and miniver, and Sir Bevis by her side. If they had vanished like two phantoms, it would have been less of a surprise than their appearance. Felicia had said no word to me of coming, and that she would come I had never anticipated. She was perfectly calm and self-possessed, and was looking extraordinarily handsome—every day lately had helped to restore her beauty—with a difference, of course; she could never be again the blithe May-rose Felicia, that Prince Charming had adored, but she was a distinguished and very lovely woman to her dying day.

"I knew you would vex yourself if you did not see me, Clare, so here I am," said she; and pointing Sir Bevis to lie down in the window-bay, she took her usual low chair, and her place by the fire, adding as she did so: "What scores of times have I sat here, Clare, talking of what has come to nothing, and you, with all the patience in the world, lending me your ears. Poor ears! how they will ache for my voice before I sit here again!"

"That will they, indeed, Felicia! But you will not be long—you will not be able to keep away from Stoneleigh."

"I shall have to stay for an invitation—have I not abdicated in favour of papa and Lady Augusta?"

She had, indeed:—"But your abdication need not be exile," I said.

"I shall be able to tell you better next year, at this time, Cousin Clare. To hear papa and my Lady talk they will not spend their charms on this country neighbourhood too often. But the Dower House will be open to me while grannie lives, and we shall visit Bylands. Papa means to exercise the rights of a tenant at the Manor, only living rent-free. George is extremely generous, and assures me that I shall always do what I like with my own." She claspt her hands on her knees, gazed absently into the fire, and neither of us spoke again for some minutes.

There are times in life when friends, the dearest

and closest, are at a loss what to say to each other, and yet silence is full of pain. Felicia had the best courage of us two; she broke it first.

"My eyes must have been dazzled with finery; you look such a little soft brown mouse, in your old merino, Clare," said she, with a half smiling, half melancholy, affectionate regard.

"If I had dreamed that you would come, I would have made myself gay, not to be so out of suit with the occasion."

"Never mind! I think I like you best as you are. I am glad too, now, that you did not come to my wedding—this is a rest. I shall believe that whatever happens, you may be found in your inch-square parlour, wearing your old brown dress; and the recollection of your douce, dear phiz, will be a comfort to me often, when I am out of your sight and out of your mind. I suppose that life, on the whole, is very dull, after one is married?"

"That depends—are you led to the philosophical reflection by the sight of me?"

"No; by general observation—life never seems dull with you: dulness is not an external accident, perhaps.—Poor grannie fainted in church—they said it was the cold. I wished her to stay away, but she fancied that would be a dereliction of duty. —We had some conversation last night together; she confessed that she had done foolishly, and I forgave her. We all need to be forgiven, Clare."

"Yes. And your papa, how has he seemed through this happy day's work?"

"Papa! oh! conscience will never trouble *him*. He is satisfied—he is at ease. He retains the Manor, Lady Augusta has a liberal fortune, and since he has done so well for himself, all men speak well of him again.—But grannie is in real grief—she will miss me when I am gone, and she is *sorry*. You must go as often as you can, and talk kindly to her, Clare. The time for reproaches is past, and you must try to console her."

I promised my darling that I would carry out her behest at the Dower House as far as my powers went, and inquired if she had any codicil to add to her will concerning her poor pensioners in the village. She could remember nothing omitted — baby Burt and his wool socks were already specially recommended to my watchfulness. When this was said I could think of no more to say, except what *yet* I did not realize: "So, Felicia, you are *married!*"

"*Married!*" echoed she. "Mrs. Sylvester-Constable of Wych-Elm—no more Miss Barrington of Stoneleigh!" After a pause, with slow reluctant movements, but a steady voice, she added: "I have a commission for you, Clare—you see this packet; it is *his* letters, and what Rosy called his 'poor little love-gift.' George's wife ought not to treasure them—and yet I could not put them in the fire. Will you take them, and destroy them or return them as you judge fit? You will know which to do when you see him——"

"I think, Felicia, we will not mention anything about them;—they should have been given back, if at all, when your engagement was broken—let them be forgotten now."

"You know best. And the chain and locket?"

"I will keep the packet as you have made it up, until you come next to the Manor."

"So be it, prudent little Clare." She followed me with her eyes wistfully while I deposited it in a safe drawer of my davenport; and then she began to say that she must go—only her grandmamma and Janet knew of her coming.

While we were still lingering and reiterating our last words, the active step of George Sylvester rang in the hall.

"Ah! runaway, here you are!" cried he, entering gay and triumphant. Felicia received him with a bright smile.

Happiness and frosty weather matched George's hale young English face, and in his sable-lined travelling-coat he looked quite imposing. It had never struck me before what a fine tall frame he was of, and what a promise he showed of squirearchal weight, bloom, and dignity for his middle-age; every year made him more and more like his father, who was a pattern for squires. Perhaps I had not considered George at his real value yet—or was it that now I wished to exalt him for

Felicia's sake? I had not, indeed, thought him worthy of her—how was it I said to myself, as there they stood before me, that but for certain sad, invincible recollections, they might have been called well-yoked? I did say so, and felt how reasonable and even desirable the marriage must appear to Felicia's other friends, who had not my prejudice, or my knowledge of the truth.

George had come to hurry his bride away. The carriage was waiting — everybody, he said, was waiting, armed with old shoes to throw after them for luck. And in a very few minutes we had kissed, shaken hands, and Felicia was gone!

The bells, which had been silent for a little while, burst out again with a prodigious din. Then there was a cheer, another and another, and the carriage with four grey horses, postilions in scarlet and wedding-favours all point-device, rolled rapidly by under our garden-hedge, and was soon out of sight.

I had nothing to do then but to sit and think, wishing for Arthur's return, or for Helen to come and tell me how it had all happened. If I had been wicked in staying away, now ensued my penalty in curiosity disappointed. Mr. Cartwright wanted to be home before dusk, and allowed Helen no time for confidences; and before we had a chance of meeting again, the event had become rather old, and I had learnt from other people every detail of the day. It had been just like other grand wedding-days in grand houses, and had gone off without any incident essential to be recorded.

CHAPTER XI.

REPENTING AT LEISURE.

A HAPPY marriage is the appropriate and natural end of most romances. People in general called the marriage of the beautiful Miss Barrington a happy marriage. But happy or not, it was only an episode in her history, and the prelude to her sharpest trial. I have said how thoroughly I disliked it; yet I was glad of the relief to my feelings which that glimpse of her with George gave me, and glad to hear the voices of congratulation that rose on all sides. Helen quite scouted the idea that it could turn out a mistake. She declared that there was no sophistry in Felicia's character, and that having given her vows to George, she would bend her mind to her duty, and learn to love him as a good wife should love a good husband. I knew my darling's intentions were excellent—what I feared was, something arising to contravene them, and to defeat her pure, affectionate purpose. But never did I admit it! Rosy Bethell challenged me once to say whether I did not think her cousin Felicia had done madly to marry George, while her heart and imagination still cherished a dear regret; but I refused to speak on the matter at all with her. I said that since Felicia was a wife, it was dangerous to be discussed, and those who loved her would hold the subject sacred. Miss Falkner was the only person besides whom I heard express an adverse opinion.

"I was rather sorry to hear of that marriage," she said in a musing, meditative way, the first time we met after the event. "Miss Barrington was made for higher things. Mr. George Sylvester is a worthy young fellow, but it was impossible he could be her absolute choice. One does not like to see such a woman accept a lower lot than she was born for. Captain Gresham is a vast friend of my brother Bob—we all like him at our house. I was perplexed to understand why he did not push his suit again when he knew she was free. I think she would not have said him Nay—and I fancy he had a fight with himself, and a very severe fight too, before he left England. Was it pride, vindictiveness, or that they really made him believe at Ringwood that she was mad? That story of her being out of her mind, while he was in India, was very cruel and mischievous. Still, as she was said to have lost her wits for his sake, he would have done more generously to have taken her back—don't you think so, Mrs. Gower?"

"I am not interested now to solve the mystery of his conduct," said I, discouragingly. "It does not matter what his motives may have been, and as I don't know what they were, I cannot condemn them—they were probably mixed, like other people's motives. Felicia is married, and the best thing we can any of us do is to forget that she ever loved anybody but her husband."

Miss Falkner acquiesced: "Yes, the shorter all

memories are now for that bit of tragedy the better—it *was* a tragedy."

Yes. I often think that Felicia's love-story was one of the saddest I ever knew.

The young couple did not go abroad after their marriage. George had no taste for foreign scenery or foreign cities. It was deep winter besides, and one's own fireside at that season is the most comfortable place. They were established at Wych-Elm when my darling wrote me her first letter—as pleasant a letter, I think, as ever I had from her.

"Here we are, dear Clare, at home under our own roof-tree, married folks of a fortnight old, sitting down to our *tête-à-tête* for life. It is a serious business to think of, but we fortify our minds by contemplating the good comradeship of other loving couples whom we know, and by promising ourselves that we shall emulate them by-and-by. George has a thousand things to amuse and occupy him here, so I am glad we came; but there has been no hunting yet because of the frost. The lake in front of the house is hard frozen, and there, at this moment, is my dear lord and master skating with the curate's pupils, —the biggest boy, the most graceful, energetic skater of any.

"We shall have enough to do at Wych-Elm as the year advances. George used to tell us that his Essex Manor House was as perfect as ours, but that was a little *ruse* of his, to make me jealous. There is this difference—the house at Stoneleigh stands on the upper slope of a long hill, and looks far and wide over a beautiful, undulating country, rich and wooded; and the house here stands on a dead flat. The trees, very fine trees, beech and elm mostly, are too close about it; and for our pretty river, we have nothing but a vast weedy pond, which will not be so cheerful presently as it is now, while frozen over. The house itself is large, too large, and has interminable stairs and corridors, and to every room an ante-room—I wish we could abolish one half of them—a house not easy to set before your mind's eye as a house to live in but a picturesque and stately house seen from a distance in the landscape. Whether summer will brighten it I don't know, but it is George's home, and therefore I mean to learn to love it. It will be a long while before I am friends with our people here as I was with my own at Stoneleigh—they are too near town for rusticity. The old landowners have migrated to more remote pastures, but the new settlers are said to be cultivated, wealthy, and sociable. George considers it a good neighbourhood. I suppose we shall be called upon soon—I am interested to know my *entourage*. If I do not like it, there is one consolation—we are within a morning's drive of London, and can go there the oftener to divert our melancholy.

"Write to me soon, like a dear little good brown mouse, and tell me *everything*."

. . . . .

The everything I had to tell my darling was only the usual village gossip, in which, however, her interest always continued. She held the same cheerful tone in her succeeding letters as she had held in the first;—perhaps she was tiring a little, but of that I thought nothing. It is so common in the newness of married life for the wife to be dull, when separated by distance from the scenes and friends of her maiden-days. It is a very pretty sentiment that the *one* person should make up for the loss of all others, but practically it is not often that he does.

"Judicious Clare, what a dear little motherly letter was that I received to-day! I handed it across the breakfast-table to George. Says George: 'I did not think Mrs. Gower had been so good a friend of mine.' Dear George! Why has it been settled by public opinion that George is not *clever?* He is not given to art, science, or literature, it is true, but he is great at all manner of sport; and I assure you he is as *deep* as anybody: shrewd, subtle, sensitive, and full of tact—as good as gold too. I am afraid, Clare, that I am sometimes a little trying both to him and myself. Satan finds some mischief still for idle hands to do! It is not very lively at Wych-Elm. I wish you lived at our gate here, that I might run in to you, and cleanse my bosom of *ennui*, that perilous stuff which weighs so heavily on modern country life! George has gone to the Meet; it is a fine hunting-day—a southerly wind and a cloudy sky. There are tufts of snowdrops in clefts of the beech-roots, so spring is coming—oh! Spring, come quickly! I have found here no musical soul yet to be congenial with; but I sing to myself half the day, and make out melodies for beautiful words that I love. And I have added some winter vignettes to my illustrated journal. It will be a great pleasure to go to London by-and-by when the concerts begin, and the picture-galleries open—I am quite looking forward to it. We have dined with our nearest neighbours, and have given our return dinners—I am thankful these first solemnities are well over. Since the frost broke, George has hunted on every hunting-day, and has been as happy as a king."

"It was rather long for a winter-day's work, and we had not above three hours to spend with dear old grandmamma, but George and I went to

Hampton Court last Wednesday. Grannie wrote that she very much wished to make George's acquaintance, and the kind, dear boy, immediately gave up his ride with the hounds to go. What would he not give up, if only he could be sure I was content? O, Clare, I am a restless spirit! not half deserving of my good fortune.

"The weather was propitious for the excursion, and we set off on the spur of the moment. At the station in London we fell in with Uncle Ralph going down too, and we all travelled together. He gave me news of papa, such news as papa never touches on himself—the preliminaries of his wedding, and so forth. George and I do not intend to be there. I cannot muster courage for that ordeal—it *would* be an ordeal. I try to harden myself, but it is a pain to think how little we shall ever be to each other again. Rosy reminds me that, in fact, I never was necessary to papa—but he was necessary to me.

"Grannie was pleased with us; I looked my best to gratify her, and George is gay without effort. She had much to ask concerning papa and his Lady Augusta, whom she has not seen yet, and was very searching in her inquiries of my affairs. She forgets nothing. But I hope I have acquired discretion; for I left her quite happy about all of us. When people rally a woman on being philosophical, they mean that she has passed under the harrow of disappointment, and escaped from the discipline in a defiant, devil-may-care humour—eh? 'My dear Felicia has become a perfect philosopher! who would have thought it once?' cried grannie, in reply to some bravado speech that I made. I was overcome with sudden confusion; Uncle Ralph set his eyes on my burning face: George reddened for sympathy—*he* makes no pretence to philosophy; and for all my endeavours, it has not yet dyed me skin deep.

"Grannie wanted sadly to have me to herself for awhile, but I would not indulge her. I knew what she would revert to, and I am purposed not to open that ghost-chamber in my life any more—have I not given George the key? Poor George, I vext him this morning before he went out, and now I am sorry! Oh, Clare, who can be always wise? Sometimes a strong caprice seizes me when I could quarrel with a straw; and it is cruel; for he is most kind and forbearing. Have you heard that Captain Gresham is returning to England soon? I pray from my heart that we may never meet! I have many a wrestle with myself when I am tempted to cry out that Cousin Clare was right in warning me against this precipitate marriage—when I would give the world it were undone! Heigho! for my good resolutions! Here am I doing the very thing I promised not to do. Forgive me, Clare, or if you cannot forgive, pity me!"

Poor darling, pity her! Indeed, I did. Forgive her!—what had I to forgive? All her wrongs were against herself. How hurt, how grieved I was by her confession, how I wished she had refrained from it! But there it was before my eyes, the fulfilment of my worst fear. What trouble it gave me to write to her kindly and firmly on the irrevocableness of her position, and the necessity of a true Christian philosophy to support it. Her answer was in her original tone of cheerful confidence, and what could she have said to make me so gravely earnest? She had evidently forgotten, and henceforward I determined to pass lightly over the hysterical cries of her old sorrow, and make as if it were dead.

But somehow, the world had got a glimpse behind the scenes now, and its idle tongues began to wag of serious domestic dissensions at Wych-Elm. I utterly refused to believe a word of them —or, at least, to admit my belief. Felicia's letters fell off in length, gradually. I could not say that they were written with effort, but they lost the easy, flowing, conversational style of her former correspondence. Her interest in her surroundings diminished instead of increasing. She gave me no view of her life, of her home, or her new circle of neighbours, who never became more than empty names to me. She mentioned her husband often, but always as "George," and she grew more and more impatient for the opening of the London season.

The marriage of Mr. Barrington and Lady Augusta was celebrated at Lowndes in March. The Manor was shut up since Felicia's own wedding, and we did not hear that its doors were soon to be re-opened. Mr. Barrington had proposed a little apartment in Paris to begin with, and Lady Augusta, who was heart and soul for gaiety and pleasure, welcomed the suggestion. So far as we could tell Judd was master at the Manor, and Arthur said often that he took far more upon him than his office justified. But there was nobody with authority to call him to account. Mr. Tom Bethell was for ever riding over to take a look round, as he said, and he tried once or twice to interfere with some arrangement of Judd's, but the man took high ground with him, and declared that he was answerable to no one but Mr. Barrington.

There was frequent grumbling in the village at the agent's encroachments and exactions, but he was ready to be insolent even to Arthur when remonstrated with; and as Arthur could appeal only to his good-feeling in these matters, and could not enforce amendment, the little troubles which make all the difference between a happy community and a discontented one, went fast from bad to worse. One day we heard that Widow Burt was to be put out of her house and field, to make a place, with the addition of the Ings below the bridge, not the common Ings, for Judd's brother. The old woman came to the Rectory in sore grief and anger, and in the impulse of the moment, I wrote off the whole story to Felicia.

Her answer showed me what a gulf she had sought to fix between the past and the present.

"Tell Grandmother Burt that if she will come and bring the boy to Wych-Elm, we will give her a pretty new lodge at our gates to live in. At Stoneleigh I can do nothing for her. It never occurred to me that any of the old cottagers would be put out of their homes. I ceded my power and property there to papa for his life, with a few restrictions in favour of the labouring poor, and let him waste it or husband it, I can do nothing."

Widow Burt, however, said she was too old to move; she must die amongst friends and neighbours where she had lived, and Arthur found her shelter on one of the Glebe farms, where, but for the change, she was not ill off.

One day, while it was still winter, the dowager drove to Stoneleigh, and went over the empty house. Afterwards she came in to visit me, leaving Miss Lassells in the Manor garden. The old lady was in a sad humour, and full of complainings. Why had Felicia permitted herself to be set aside, as she had done? she ought not to have delegated her duties to anyone. It was easy to be foreseen that Mr. Barrington would not reside at the Manor, by whatever plausible pretences he had won her over; he would spend the whole income of the property elsewhere, and what better would it be for the mere name of a squire? Why, as she drove along the road by the new copses which Tom Bethell had caused to be planted, she saw that the oak-fencing was broken down in no less than four places! Judd must be plundering the property finely, and neglecting it as well. Ah! things had been so different in her dear Wilfred's time—Felicia was much to blame for relinquishing her rights and duties to her extravagant, careless father, and his frivolous wife.

"It seems to me that Mr. Barrington has always done whatever he pleased both with Felicia and with what belongs to her," said I. "A woman's rights are limited practically by the honour and uprightness of the men she loves:—father, husband, brother, son, it matters not which; if they be violent and greedy, and she forbearing, she gives them up what they want. The law can help her at her appeal, but imagine Felicia appealing to the law!"

"Of course, she never would—she never ought, Some men are just—not many. Poor Felicia has been very unhappy. However, she is in the hands of a good man now. George is not clever, but he is a kind fellow."

I asked the dowager if she was anticipating a visit from the young couple by-and-by.

"No," she said. "They have several plans, but not one of them includes Gladeshire. Felicia mentions that she will time her coming to meet her father's—but when will that be, who can tell?

I suppose they will be in London through the season. Felicia is preparing to enter with zest into its pleasures now—a married woman has so much more liberty than a girl. And I think she is as beautiful as ever—more beautiful in some respects. George must be very proud of her. I wish I could be sure she loves him."

"She does love him, she honours and respects him," said I, firmly.

"Ah, yes, she could not do otherwise; but that is not quite what I mean—*you know*."

Yes, I knew, but what need to say so; best be silent now on all that; best let the dead past bury its dead. I spoke of the long habit of fondness and affection which had subsisted between George and Felicia, as a fair foundation for conjugal peace. The old lady listened, and was a little relieved, but it was with a very wistful look that she rejoined:—

"You live out of the world—you know nothing of its perils, excitements, temptations."

I smiled in her face, and said: "I trust never to know anything."

"You have no fear, then, for Felicia?—so impetuous, yet so weak, so passionate and sudden."

"No fear at all. She bears a conscience. She may suffer more yet, but she will never do wrong wilfully. She is a better woman than any of us know. She is purposed to do right, and God keeps a hold over such."

"Dear Mrs. Gower, you remember that we have heard her *doubt*."

"God is constantly before her eyes for all that. I have no fear for my darling—but if evil could befall her, I should still say that she was more sinned against than sinning."

"You have not been told that she and George are reported *not* to get on well together?" inquired the old lady, with visible hesitation.

"If I were told so, and if I believed it, I should only make light of it," said I, diplomatically. "The beginning of many people's married life is difficult. I have only to look back at my own—how fractious I was, how exacting and perverse; we might have been miserable for life, if Arthur had not been able to manage me. It is a pet theory of mine that a young wife is pretty much what her husband has the wit to make her. George knows all; there is no secret between Felicia and himself. He loves her with magnanimity, and will earn her true devotion—that is my faith for them both."

"May you prove a just discerner! But there is a worse danger—even before the marriage it was said to me, that Captain Gresham had sworn to make her repent her rejection of him in every vein of her heart."

"Nonsense! I will not credit it—besides she has done it already, and that act of her tragedy is over. The very expression betrays to me that it came, not from his lips, but from her own—I have heard her use it. It is a very old phrase—that he would make his enemies bleed in every vein of their hearts, was a common threat of one of our vindictive old kings—Edward IV. or Henry VIII., I forget which. We must not be too credulous; and we must not be the first to give ear and currency to idle tales that may lead to mischief.

Felicia is married now, and her chief desire is to be a good wife to George; and I feel quite sure that she will compass it in the end."

"I wish I had your implicit confidence—but I fear it is based on a blissful ignorance of what ordinary men and women are made of," said the dowager.

"I do not pretend to a very deep or wide knowledge—in fact, I have often wondered how it is that I come in contact with no *bad* people, when the earth is currently reported to be overrun with them! I observe that human nature is strong, and that to guide it is safer than to thwart, deny or crush it. I observe also that temptation does not make us evil, but only shows us what we are. Would you call Felicia and Captain Gresham of the common run?—I have been used to think of them as much more than that. In both there is a root of honour and goodness which temptation will not pluck up. What of their passion lives on, I cannot say—I dare not assert that it is extinct."

"I did very foolishly in helping to divide them! It was my fault. I should have supported her—

Lucilla disappointed my ambition: it revived again for Felicia, to be again how cruelly overthrown! If she had married Captain Gresham, he has at least the name that he is *somebody*—as for poor George he is *nobody*."

"George is a worthy and excellent gentleman, as tender of his good repute as any *somebody* that ever stept, and with a heart to be wrung, like any other good man's. Let by-gones be by-gones! Give up fearing for Felicia—it is a shame to doubt her."

This was the only thing I could reiterate by way of fulfilling my darling's directions to comfort her grandmamma. It was the Ringwood people who infused these distressful anxieties into her mind. If this should happen, if that should happen! I have known persons who revelled in imaginary disasters for their friends as unctuously as if they were anticipating some great benefit for themselves. Rosy Bethell had a large and increasing gift that way, and compassionated her Cousin Felicia now as openly as she had once caluminated her.

"Poor Cousin Felicia, I wish she may not find that she has married in haste to repent at leisure! George and she agree like fire and water," was her method of allusion; and then she would look as absurdly dejected as Miss Colquhoun, grimacing over an incorrigible navvy, shaking her head with an affectation of concern that provoked me cruelly.

Helen also had heard the two rumours which the dowager recited to me—Captain Gresham's threat of revenge, and the failure of harmony between George and Felicia. She would not say that she absolutely discredited either. There was no improbability in them to her mind—not even in the threat. Paul, she said, was mixed of good and evil, like other men—there was bitterness in his heart, and there might be vindictiveness in his passion, and no pity now—but she had confidence in Felicia; and this consoled me.

It was observed that Squire Sylvester, after a short visit to Essex in April, no longer spoke spontaneously of his son George's wonderful good-fortune, but contented himself with answering simply to the inquiries of neighbours. Felicia's letters gave no hint of disagreement since her first confession, and surely, I thought, her pen in writing would betray unhappy feeling if any existed. On the whole, the rumours of quarrels and menace did not much trouble me. But I know nothing positive of these early months of her married life save what she told me herself, and that was not much. We were soon, however, to have a reporter on the scene in Rosy Bethell, who during the winter manœuvred seriously but unsuccessfully for an invitation to Wych-Elm. If any dissension did prevail there, Felicia exercised a sound discretion in not asking Rosy for a witness of it.

Rosy, verging towards thirty, had arrived at the conclusion that it was not her vocation to marry, but to be a good lady, and mend her fellow-creatures. It was now finally arranged that she should leave Ringwood, and Miss Reed with her, as companion—how delighted the young ones were at that exodus! A pretty residence near Gladestone was first thought of, but, prompted by Miss Reed, Rosy felt that she should be in a wider sphere of usefulness if she lived in London. To London, therefore, they went, and established themselves in a small new house at Kensington, before the season began, to be in readiness for the May Meetings, and other religious and benevolent transactions, which they entered into as part of their business. They made themselves luxuriously comfortable, according to Mr. Tom Bethell's account, and as he went often to his favourite daughter, and stayed long, no doubt it was a literal fact. The brown-bread and water-cress diet of old Mrs. Clarissa Constable was much too ascetic for pious ladies of Miss Colquhoun's type, whom Rosy more nearly resembled—and besides, Miss Reed was perfectly devoted to her ease, and would not have proved an amiable yoke-fellow to any patroness who did not make good living a primary consideration.

Felicia's own house in London was still occupied by the tenant to whom it had been leased before her coming of age; but the house where Mrs. Clarissa Constable had lived in dust and decay, from her husband's death to her own, was in a tolerable quarter of the town, and George had it renovated for his wife's occupation. Rosy called upon them the day after they went into it, condoled with Felicia on its antiquated dimness, and invited her to lunch at Kensington on the morrow, that she might show her what a charming modern residence she had acquired. Felicia regretted that she must decline Rosy's hospitality; her engagements were so many that she had not a free day for a month.

"You *are* living at a pace! I pity George!" was Rosy's comment on the occasion.

"I suppose it is the pace everybody lives at who lives in gay London society, and they get used to it, like any other labour, going through their day's work and night's work of visiting and entertaining as systematically as workers for bread go through theirs—and not toiling much less severely perhaps," was Felicia's careless answer.

Rosy deduced from it that all her gaiety and going about failed to satisfy her Cousin Felicia, and this was the burden of her first letter from London to me. Rosy initiated the correspondence herself, and as she did not exact a reply to more than one letter in three, we kept it up for several years, and only dropt it when we had no longer the sole subject of interest between us, my dear Felicia, to write about.

The Pharisee's famous thankgiving to God for his superiority over other men was curiously, almost ludicrously parodied in some of these early epistles of Rosy's. She was for ever striking an attitude, and comparing her life and conversation with Felicia's—and always to Felicia's disadvantage. To me her new zeal, her spiritual conceit, and false humility were a jest; but when Arthur studied her letters, he said there was a real intention of sincerity in them—she believed that she had chosen a better way than the way of the world, and she was trying to walk in it. He would not let me call her *hypocrite,* though she wore her religiousness yet more as an outer garment than as an inner principle; she was self-deceiving to a great degree, but not a wilful pretender to virtues that she had not; and with more knowledge, especially more self-knowledge, he maintained that she might become in truth what she was yet only in aspiration—a helpful, useful woman.

Poor Rosy, she embarked on her good life in London with all the audacity of inexperience, and no miracle was worked to save her from its natural results. The humiliating accidents and misadventures that befel her at the very outset could not but bear some fruit of wholesome instruction. For a few months, while April, May and June were on the wing, she had a favourite, unfailing theme of grave detraction in Felicia's extravagance in trifles, her waste of money over pretty things, and especially over flowers for the decoration of her dull rooms; and in July, behold Rosy herself was found in debt, which she could not pay, and fell thereupon into dire confusion and distress!

"We have a man in plain clothes, and four maids—three of them Christians," she had told me in describing her establishment, adding that she had bought her carriage but jobbed her horses, on account of the trouble and inconvenience which often occurred when no more than a pair were kept. At the time Arthur and I remarked that her income must be at least double what we supposed, if it could support that rate of expenditure in London. The fact was that, living always as a guest before, she had acquired no knowledge of how far money would go, and too wise in her own conceit to ask information, she framed her affairs on a scale which four times her means would not bear, and the very first quarter left her in difficulties. Though neither of them told me, I know that Felicia came to the rescue, and saved her from serious mortifications, but it was impossible to save her from all. The charming new house at Kensington had to be exchanged for an apartment in Manchester Square, the man, the carriage, the horses and two of the maids had to be dispensed with, and Rosy had to economize on ready money for a long while after her brief excursion into the regions of unlimited credit. She would have returned to Ringwood in her fright, but Mrs. Bethell set her face steadfastly against that; and in her diminished fortunes, Miss Reed did not display the sympathy that might have been expected in so old a hanger-on of the family. She adhered to these diminished fortunes it is true, but she reminded Rosy often that she could place herself much more comfortably than in Manchester Square, and Rosy did not pluck up spirit to bid her go and do it, then, as she was advised. Rosy was one of those spasmodically energetic characters who are invariably ruled by somebody, and, perhaps, it was as well Miss Reed should rule her as another. The family were of that opinion —only outsiders suggested that she should get rid of her tyrant.

It seemed a singular irony of fortune that her Cousin Felicia, whom Rosy never heartily loved, whom she had envied and injured, should be the one only person who showed her kindness and consideration in her misfortunes. Even her father was angry, and said she had deceived him about the carriage and the man-servant—he had assured her they were impossible on her income, and yet in direct defiance of his counsel and experience, she had set about trying to keep them. Then her sister Blanche, Mrs. Courtney, intimated that she did not intend Rosy to come sponging and preaching in her house, where *riz-de-veau-aux-champignons* was a very rare delicacy indeed. This cutting allusion was aimed at the confectioner's bills delivered on Rosy's catastrophe, in which that costly dainty figured more extensively than any other. It appeared that Miss Reed had a weakness for it—Rosy pleaded even with tears that mutton-broth would content her, but what could she do? Reed adored her dinner—it was the one pleasure in life left her.

The removal into Manchester Square brought Rosy into Felicia's neighbourhood, and, in the kindness of her heart, Felicia used to call for her of an afternoon to drive in the Park or elsewhere often, and in many ways made up to her for the straitnesses to which she was temporarily reduced. Even a share of beautiful flowers fell to Rosy, and then she learnt that instead of being a lavish bi-weekly purchase, as she had assured me, they were sent regularly from Wych-Elm with fruit, vegetables, and other country produce, a liberal supply of which began to find its way to her own larder.

"I do not know how we should get on at all comfortably but for Cousin Felicia, who is, I think, the most generous creature that ever lived," she now wrote. "She even brought poor old Reed one of her sweet-bread and mushroom tarts the other day, brought it herself in the carriage—was it not thoughtful and good of her, knowing how partial Reed is to nice eating? Poultry is immensely dear in London, but Felicia often sends us Wych-Elm chicken, and when papa was in town last week, she took care that we should have everything he likes. She calls me a miserable housekeeper; I am afraid I have no head for management, and if I leave it to Reed, she would sacrifice all else, even appearances, to spreading our table as if we were aldermen. Felicia has so much money at command that she can afford whatever she pleases; but I wish, poor thing, she were happier in her life, and George too."

In answering this letter, I said to Rosy that I hoped her fancies about Felicia's unhappiness were as mistaken as her fancies about the flowers. But I had heard from other quarters by this time, that my darling was very restless, excitable and capricious. She was having a triumphant season as a beautiful bride; she was to be seen everywhere where the rich, gay, and fashionable most did congregate; no grand assembly was complete without her presence; no amateur concert was a success without her voice. Her husband was constant in his attendance upon her, and did his best to look as if he were in his element, and enjoying what she enjoyed. But the effort was visible enough to those who knew him. George was bored, but he did his duty; for wherever Felicia appeared, there appeared Captain Gresham, haunting her like her shadow; still friendly, with his old friend George, who was friendly also with him, but marked by sneering eyes of the world, and whispered about by its evil tongues.

Some persons have expressed surprise that George Sylvester permitted, and apparently did not discourage, the renewal of their intimacy. He had a perfect confidence in his wife, and no distrust of his friend. Perhaps he hoped by this means to exorcise old memories and phantoms which

Felicia still unmarried, and to make her more entirely his own. He succeeded in the end, it is true, but not without passing through a terrible ordeal—not until they had all been tried as by fire. Or perhaps, and this is more probable, he suffered temporarily what he could not have hindered, save by a violent exercise of authority. He was in the midst of the coil, and knew its knots; I am willing to believe that he saw best how it might be unwound and disentangled. George never appeared blameable to me.

CHAPTER XII.

TRIED AS BY FIRE.

It is not my intention to linger over this tragical chapter of Felicia's story. It will be understood as well told briefly as told at length. I was not witness to it, nor have I a single letter of the date. Mrs. Clarissa Constable's words came true. In her greatest temptation and greatest sorrow God let her find no helper, no comforter, but in Himself.

The first meeting of the unhappy lovers, as it was related to me, took place at Kingston House in the month of May, at one of those gatherings to which flock a crowd of all manner of people, from royal dukes to poor poets, artists and professionals, who have plucked a single leaf of laurel, and aspire some day to be crowned. Such as loved conversation and to stare at each other chiefly, circulated in the *salon*, but the select *habitués* gravitated to the music-room, and on this sad, memorable night, there, amongst the rest, was Felicia with her friend Sophie, Mrs. Cadogan, their German master, now established in fame and fortune, and a young Italian singer, preparing for his *début*.

Rosy Bethell professed to have quite renounced the world, but she saw no harm yet in a concert, a flower-show, or a *soirée*, and occasionally, to brighten her monotonous evenings before her removal from Kensington, Felicia would carry her to some entertainment whither she and George were going. Kingston House was a decidedly worldly house, according to Rosy's views, but she had a curiosity to see it, if only for once, and this was the occasion she chanced upon. Rather shy of the novel and mixed society, she clung close to her cousin, and followed her to the music-room, where she found a safe corner to shelter her innocence in a cushioned window-seat. Mrs. Cadogan, Mrs. Mellish and the German master sang to an audience in perpetual movement; only George, propping one of the door-posts, was a fixture.

"I will not stay late—don't go out of sight," was Felicia's constant promise, and injunction; and George signified his acquiescence, though his wife's practice was to stay *very* late. Whatever differences of sentiment might occur between them in private, in public George was most patiently devoted. No one manifested a more genuine pleasure than he when his wife sang, sang exquisitely, and was applauded with polite enthusiasm.

The first notes of Felicia's voice brought a multitude of hearers from the *salon*, and in the rear rank of them, Rosy, to her sudden astonishment, perceived Captain Gresham. For a few moments she did not recognize him with certainty; his beard, his darkened complexion, and the interval since she had seen him, had added twice that number of years to his appearance. He had the air of thirty, she thought. He listened, watching Felicia till her song was finished, and then disappeared in the crowd; but as if drawn back by an irresistible attraction, he returned when the music recommenced.

This time the young Italian was performing with outrageous gestures, feigning and fancying a world more than he had passion to express. Felicia was standing beside her husband, her hand resting on his arm, and looking lovely, exalted, inspired, as she always did with music in her ears. Their recognition of Captain Gresham was simultaneous. George did not look forbidding, Felicia blushed, and held faster to George; but her eyes, like the eyes of a fascinated bird, had met the gaze of her former lover, and were not withdrawn.

"A soul in pain, that was what she made me think of," said Rosy. "If I could read her face, she was entreating him to pass by, and not to speak to them; but he advanced, and George and he shook hands, like friends who have not met for an age: They remained together the rest of the evening, chatting as freely as if Captain Gresham were anybody else. But the burning spot never left Felicia's cheek, nor the wild entreaty her eyes. Captain Gresham said he had only crossed from France a few days before, and his sister was gone down to Harrow, to see her boys."

A soul in pain! my poor lost darling!

This encounter was the renewal of sorrow. The next day, in the Park, there by Felicia's carriage rode Captain Gresham, not in the crowd, but beyond the fashionable mile where witnesses were not so many. Mr. Ralph Barrington extending his constitutional walk in the same direction was overtaken by them, and on recovering from his shock of amazement, he asked Felicia to give him a few turns in the ring as she had a vacant seat. Rosy was her only companion that day. Captain Gresham made his bow presently, and rode off, and then Felicia's uncle, peering at her with his keen, cold eyes, said he thought that gentleman had been still abroad. Felicia coloured under his scrutiny, and gave all the explanation she had it in her power to give, to which her Uncle Ralph rejoined: "You begin to know the world as well as I know it; so I will not intrude my advice upon you;" but his tone was significant of warning that the less she was seen in public with Captain Gresham the better for all concerned.

That evening George and Felicia were at the opera, and in a stall behind them sat Captain Gresham. They chatted between the acts, went away together, and appeared on excellent terms to those who saw them with interest. Any surprise that might have been excited was soon forgotten, and it became a common remark that if Mrs. Sylvester-Constable was at any entertainment, there be sure was Captain Gresham too. Of course it was not always the case, but it was frequent enough to justify the gossips in asserting it. Mrs. Mellish had a wicked delight in studying what she called the progress of their *intrigue*, and her husband was said to have a bet upon its conclusion — it might be true; there is no honest friendship in such people. Mrs. Mellish had been talked about herself, and acquitted; she was a very clever little woman, but Felicia had too much heart to escape so easily from the scathe of tongues. All her sad story was known, and it was a jest, or a very pitiful story, according to the mind of each person who heard it.

Mr. Barrington and Lady Augusta had been in town during the early part of the season, but had gone to Spa since, and were there at this moment: a long way off, but by no means out of hearing of fashionable scandal. Lady Augusta affected a kind, persuasive, elder-sisterly tone with her step-daughter, and from her came a gentle word of counsel and caution very skilfully put. Felicia was set on her guard against herself, and not offended. She went to Hampton Court for a few days and returned: she went to Aspencliffe and returned. "She is like a moth fluttering about a flame," was one of Rosy's phrases. It made my heart sick; it made me feel very bitter against Captain Gresham. He knew what he was doing—I was sure of that, and sure also that he was the stronger, whether for good or evil. Why did he not go out of the way? He had gone once before when he had better have stayed—had he, indeed, uttered that cruel threat, that he was torturing her, and making her a bye-word? or was he himself as blind, and weak and reckless, as she seemed?

It was now July. I wrote to my darling—it was very hard writing under such circumstances, and she answered my letter in a light, almost flippant tone—a tone so unlike her nature, that I destroyed it as soon as read. I was more disquieted than ever. If I could have seen her for an hour I should have learnt more of what she was doing, feeling, and desiring than it was possible to gather from report. One week Rosy would write that she was most brilliant and lively, the gayest of the gay, and the next that she could not tell what ailed her, but she supposed that she was unhappy.

Squire Sylvester went to town, and stayed a little while at his son's house, where he found Captain Gresham a chartered guest, coming and going at all hours. George and he had been the most intimate friends, and George did not appear to see any reason why they should not be so still.

Wiser men judged his confidence rash, to say the least of it.

The dowager heard all that was rumoured, and her imagination far out-ran the truth. "Miserable Felicia! she is bent on bringing disgrace into two honourable families! I shall never hold up my head again! But I am justly punished! She once cried out against me that I should make her a wicked woman—she is a wicked woman! She tampers with temptation when she should turn her back upon it. And he is worse. He is playing the very part of Satan; for it is out of revenge he would destroy her. He has no love for her, such as poor George has—poor fool, to trust her as he does!"

"What can Felicia mean?" said Mr. Tom Bethell, in a morose dry tone. "Her name is bandied about from lip to lip as it was two or three years ago, but with even less reverence. I have bidden Rosy leave her to herself. I will not have Rosy lightlied as her friend."

These two speeches were made me in one day—Ah! what a wretched day that was! I entreated

Arthur to bethink him of some remedy — as a minister of God, who had long had charge of Felicia's soul, could he not interfere? He said he had already determined on a step.

"Felicia has her husband—if he cannot keep her, no one can." But he would write to Captain Gresham. "Perhaps *he* will hear me—perhaps he has no friend bold enough to tell him the truth."

I saw the letter written, and when it was gone, gone with as urgent a prayer as ever rose up to heaven, I felt in my mind strangely at rest and peace.

It was only three days after (Arthur had said to me at breakfast, "They will carry the last load of corn to-day,") while walking on the hills with the children, to see the end of the harvest, that we met Captain Gresham coming up from Bylands on his way to our house. We knew him a long way off—his quick, swinging step, the whole air and manner of the man were not to be mistaken. What a cry of thanksgiving broke from my heart!

I quickened my pace; the children ran to meet him the sooner. He tossed Lizzie in the air, and kissed her as he set her down, and complimented Jack upon his manliness. There was a dreadful gaiety about him, a light, senseless mirth such as froths over some people's minds when they have escaped a danger, and have not yet had time to consider how great it was, or by what means their rescue has been effected. As for me I had no voice to greet him; I could only look up with clouded eyes, and feel supremely glad. When they cleared, I saw the changes in him, and a countenance that was a riddle. He looked haggard and weary as after vehement agitation, but though he talked carelessly of indifferent things, and made noisy sport with the children who recollected him perfectly, and would not leave him, I felt that I had no need to accuse him of want of feeling or want of heart. Whatever he had done, visibly he had suffered.

After we had walked a little while in company, he stopt short, and said that as he had met me, he would not pursue his excursion to Stoneleigh. "I was going to report myself to my spiritual commanding officer. You, as his deputy, will do as well. Tell him that he will find me at Fairfield any day after to-morrow. I broke my journey at Bylands last night."

We shook hands, and he struck off up the hill, not in the direction of Mr. Willis's house, but of the High Beech Copse. It was a beautiful afternoon, and the air was exhilarating above the valley. I think he was relieved to escape just then the sight of scenes all darkened with vain regrets. We said not a word of whence he had come, nor why; but as he left me I know my heart ached for him as much as ever it had ached for Felicia!

For a week after, wherever we went, whoever we met, we heard one announcement.

"Captain Gresham is at Fairfield—in very good time for the partridges. He looks ill, and says he has had a touch of fever—country air and diet will soon cure him;" this was Mr. Tom Bethell's shrewd remark.

"Gresham was in the Club at Gladestone to-day—we rode part of the way home together. Our people are gone down to Wych-Elm. There is nobody left in town, he says," this was Squire Sylvester's buoyant speech over our gate, between two puffs of a cigar, and he trotted off with a cheerful nod.

Everything was understood—nothing was explained. I had not had so light a spirit for many a day! What I waited and watched for still was the next letter from Felicia—yes, I was very anxious for that.

Arthur went over to Fairfield, not so soon as he was bidden, but as soon as he had the opportunity, and he brought me word that Captain Gresham was in a frantic way. From some quarter he had learnt that Felicia was ill again, "of her old complaint." Arthur asked what he meant by her old complaint, and Captain Gresham put his hand to his forehead significantly, adding, with an outburst of remorse, that he should have her death at his door—or worse—the loss of her reason! Arthur talked to him soothingly, and assured him that Felicia's reason had never really failed her before, whatever people had said.

"Are you telling me the truth?" asked Captain Gresham, with fierce suspicion.

Arthur recited to him events as they happened within our ken, and from Captain Gresham's further questions and admissions, he discovered that he had been convinced, though sorely against his will, of the calumnious lie that Ringwood had set afloat. It was his own fault.—But I could not think of that now! I could think only of my poor darling!

As we heard nothing from Wych-Elm, after the lapse of another week, I wrote to Felicia. In course of the post there came an answer, but it was from George. He seemed quite heart-broken, and begged Arthur to spare me for a few days to his dear wife.—It was impossible for Arthur to gainsay my wish to be gone.

At the Gladestone station we fell in with Mr. Tom Bethell, as cheerful as if somebody had made him a handsome present.

"You are on your road to Wych-Elm? I guessed as much," said he, and added that from what Rosy, who was there with her cousin, wrote, he feared that I should find her in a very bad way.

We had some time to wait for the train, and I inquired what Rosy's intelligence was. He gave me her letter to read in the carriage, saying that there was nothing private in it, and bidding me destroy when I had done with it. It was very long, and I was too agitated and impatient for a start to read it on the platform where we were; so I reserved it until I was by myself. Arthur travelled with me to London, and then it being Saturday, and his Sunday duty unprovided for, he returned home, and I continued my journey to Wych-Elm alone.

What I gathered from Rose Bethell's letter to her father was this, and George Sylvester, Janet and others were in the same story when we came to speak of what had happened.

On a certain night, now nearly three weeks ago, there had been a grand ball at Kingston House, for a wind-up of the season. For two or three days before Felicia had been extremely unsettled, irritable and unhappy. Captain Gresham was at the house frequently in George's absence, and always after these visits Felicia's excitability was so much increased that Janet and Carr grew alarmed for her health, and confessed to each other that they heartily wished the season were over, and their dear mistress safe again in the country.

It chanced that the very evening preceding the ball, within half-an-hour of Captain Gresham's leaving her after a prolonged visit, Dr. Gooch called. His practised observation was not at fault, and living in the world, he was probably aware of the world's talk. Felicia had long since given him the right to speak to her both as a friend and a physician, and he frankly assured her that she was quite overwrought, as well in mind as in body, that she must give herself more rest, and must go to no more late night entertainments for the present. She pleaded hard for this last ball, she could not give that up. The doctor reiterated that if she were wise, she would betake herself to pure country air and wholesome rest without a day's delay; and her husband coming in while he was still there, he repeated his advice with emphasis.

Felicia was obstinate, however. She would go to Wych-Elm *after* the ball as soon as George pleased; but unless he were very unkind, he would not insist upon her going *before*. It was not George's policy to insist on anything with her. When he could not persuade her to listen to good advice, he took pains to mitigate the consequences of her indiscretion and caprice, and being of a sanguine temper, he hoped always for the best.

It had never been Felicia's way to distress her milliner or her maids, but she was anxious to a perplexing degree that what she was to wear on the occasion of this ball should be absolutely perfect; and Janet and Carr humoured her to the doing and undoing of a dozen trimmings on a Brussels lace, and white satin slip, before she was satisfied with the effect. Rosy Bethell, who dined with her and George that evening, and saw them start for Kingston House, said that she had never seen her Cousin Felicia look more resplendently beautiful, though her eyes betrayed the wasting excitement that burnt like a fire within. Everyone guessed what anticipation it was fed the fire.

For the first time George watched her with real solicitude.

"You are not fit to go to this ball, Felicia—do be prevailed on to remain at home," he urged at the very last moment, when the carriage was at the door.

To this she replied, defiantly: "How absurd, George! I never felt in a more dancing mood than to-night!"

In a dancing mood or not, she danced very little, and at her own request George brought her away early—before midnight, and before all the company had arrived. She had an air of disappointment; her feverish excitement had vanished when she reached home, and she was shivering, pallid, and dejected.

"Take off my finery, Janet; it is the last ball to which I shall ever go!" she said, and dropt with a sick languor on her bed.

All night she tossed wakefully, or slept and dreamed by snatches. In the morning some sad expectation weighed on her which was observed. Captain Gresham had not appeared at the ball the previous night—was she watching for his coming now? She gave orders that she was at home if any one called, and in the middle of the morning the servants heard her in the drawing-room, singing, walking about, and talking. They supposed Miss Bethell to be with her, but Janet, going up by-and-by, found her alone, arranging and re-arranging her flowers.

Janet's errand was to say that blind Mary, as she was called, that pensioner of Mrs. Clarissa-Constable, who had been present in the house at the time of her death, had come to the door, and begged with great urgency to see the nephew of her old benefactress or his wife. Felicia, full of nervous impatience, inquired curtly, what did she want? Janet replied that the poor creature seemed very wretched and destitute; she had recovered the partial use of her limbs, but she trailed one foot, and she was hawking small matters of needlework to sell, illuminated Scripture texts, book-markers, and such trifles. Felicia said

Janet might buy something for half-a-crown, and send her away; she was an impostor who did not deserve encouragement. Janet went, and returned with a cross composed of graduated layers of white perforated card-board, attached to a red ribbon, for a Bible-mark. Felicia said it was prettily made, and pinned it to her side, as nuns wear a rosary; and while asking a few questions about the poor seller, her mood softened, and she promised to see her if she came again. She was in the kitchen at that moment, Janet said; the master of the house had gone out when she stood at the door, had recognized and pitied her, and ordered to give her some food. Felicia, however, declined to see her then, pleading that she was engaged.

Soon after arrived Rosy Bethell to hear about the ball, but found her cousin disinclined for conversation, and as she thought, very restless and nervous in manner. Felicia answered her direct questions, and amongst others, she answered in the negative an inquiry whether Captain Gresham was at the ball. Thereupon Rosy assumed the pathetic mission of counsellor, and said:—

"Oh, Felicia, if you could give up dwelling upon the idea of him, how much happier might your life be! You *never* will be happy, George and you, until you put Captain Gresham out of your mind!"

Instead of resenting this plain speech, Felicia answered with a faint tremulousness, that if Captain Gresham had been at the ball the night before, she had meant to bid him good-by, and never to see him again of her own good will. Here Rosy should have stopped, but with the cruelty which springs from want of tact, and the utter absence of sympathy and comprehension, she added:—

"I am glad of that; for I am convinced he is only teasing you as a cat might tease a poor bird. It flatters his vanity to hear the world say you are at his beck, but he is not prepared to throw away the world for such silliness as love—that is papa's opinion. And besides, it is *wicked*, now you are George's wife."

Felicia glanced at her strangely, toyed with the red ribbon, and, after contemplating the cross at the end of it for a few minutes in silence, raised it to her lips, and kissed it. Rosy shook her vague little head, and rebuked her for idolatry.—A few minutes after this Captain Gresham was ushered into the drawing-room. Felicia rose quickly to meet him, white as a ghost, and trembling like a leaf. Captain Gresham looked self-possessed enough as he entered, but when he took Felicia's hand, he changed colour, and his agitation became as strong as her own.

"You are very cold, and yet it is a sultry day," he said.

"You will be grateful to escape into the country; I have been expecting you to say good-by," replied Felicia, and her mournful eyes never left his face.

His fell, and fixed on the cross which she had just bought of the poor impostor. He did not contradict her words, but his countenance expressed the darkest perplexity and dismay.

Something was said of the ball, and Felicia asked why he was not there as he had promised. He answered that he had been there; and on further explanation it came out that he must have reached Kingston House just as George and she left; he said he had not gone until very late —he had been prevented. (He did not tell her as he told Arthur, whose letter he had received that morning, that the delay was caused by a battle with himself, in which, so far as *his* will went, the devil won.)

"As you have come now I do not care, but I should have been sorry not to say good-by," said Felicia, with a plaintive thrill in her voice, and tears flooding her eyes.

Captain Gresham suddenly approached her, and was beginning to speak, when she stood up too, and laid the cross that she had kissed upon his lips. He was silent. Rosy, moved by what impulse she never could tell, stole noiselessly from the room. And that saddest of partings had no witness but Him who is invisible.

A very short while after Rosy left, Captain Gresham ran downstairs, and was being let out by the butler just as the master of the house came up the steps. Captain Gresham spoke a few hurried words about leaving London that day or the next, and they separated with a grasp of the hand, George calling after his friend that if he happened to see the Squire at Gladestone, he was to tell him they were all well, and off to Wych-Elm before the week's end.

George went immediately upstairs, intending to enter the drawing-room, but heard, as he supposed, Rosy with his wife, and perhaps some other ladies, in full gossip, for there was talking and laughter both soft and continuous, and thereupon he turned back to the peace and silence of the library below, to wait till they were gone. By-and-by the butler announced luncheon on the table, and George then mounted to bring down his wife and her friend or friends, as the case might be. He went through the back drawing-room, but before he saw Felicia he discovered that she was alone—that it was her voice never ceased, her laughter that sounded so strange. She was walking about with her head thrown back, reciting to herself broken snatches of songs, interspersed with short sentences of conversation, and bursts of most joyless mirth.

"Rehearsing, Felicia! What is the play? Why, I thought you were half-a-dozen people at least!" exclaimed her husband, though a great, defined fear had laid sudden hold upon him.

She stood still, turned her head aside with a cowering motion, and put up her two hands to shield her averted face from his view. He advanced and quietly drew them down, bidding her not be so foolish, and still asking what was the play. The tears began to run from her eyes, and she answered him with incoherence, or with silence, but she was gently submissive to his commands.

A couple of hours later, by the urgent advice of Dr. Gooch, they were on their road to Wych-Elm, Janet and Carr in the closed carriage with their dear, unhappy young mistress, and her husband riding on before.

CHAPTER XIII.

"OUT OF THE DEPTHS."

A HEAVY, irregular pile of brick building, with stone dressings and a multiplicity of grotesque windows, chimney-stacks, gables, turrets, lying drowsily in the after-glow of a hot August evening—beech-trees in full suits of deep green dotting long levels of sunburnt sward—a lake dark, shadowless, motionless—a belt of flowers under the wall—that was my first impression of Wych-Elm, Felicia's married home. There was neither stir nor sound about the place, and I walked up the avenue to the great square porch without disturbing so much as a bird. There had been no carriage for hire at the station, and, as my arrival was uncertain, none had been sent to meet me; but a mile across the fields and the park, with a boy for guide, brought me safely to my journey's end.

I was just about to ring at the door when a voice cried to me not to touch the bell, and there was George Sylvester, in evening costume, smoking his after-dinner cigar. He looked out of spirits, and as he led me to the side-door from which he had come himself, he said that Felicia was very ill, and they kept the house as quiet as possible. It seemed to me more dead than alive. George thanked me warmly for responding to his summons at once, and said that Rosy Bethell had gone away only that morning, alluding to her departure as a relief. He thought Rosy did more harm than good, and I could well imagine that, knowing her school of piety.

"She babbles till Felicia frets from pure exhaustion, then she weeps too. My poor darling needs cheering, not casting down with talk of her sins and naughty heart—as sweet a heart as ever beat, God bless her! And I don't know what Rosy means by her sins—it would be a better world if everybody else was half as good! However, she is gone, and Carr and Janet expect they shall get on better."

He spoke as if the present order of things was not likely soon to change. By Dr. Gooch's directions Felicia had been exiled from her pretty decorated rooms, which had a south-western aspect, to a cool north corner of the great house, and was permitted to see no one from out of doors. George said it would not be desirable for her to see me that night, and until she was prepared, and I sufficiently rested to have my voice and feelings under control. He did not say in so many words that there was a dread lest her mind might give way, but I inferred it—indeed, I had done so already from Rosy's letter to her father, and from other rumours circulating freely in Gladeshire during the last week.

I was tired after my journey, and thankful to eat, and go to rest. The housekeeper conducted me to a vast wilderness of a room, where Carr came to me, and gave me, before I slept, a full account of how her dear lady's nervous attacks had grown from little to more, and from bad to worse, until she was now quite as ill as on a former occasion. Dr. Gooch had said that it might be necessary to watch her, and even to keep her under gentle restraint, but with care and caution, he hoped to avoid the *worst.* Janet and Carr, her two faithful servants, had the sole charge of her under the physician's instruction.

"She is that unhappy, she is a sight to *kill* them that love her," said the good nurse, wiping her eyes, which had suddenly filled with tears. "The fever has been at work for ever so long, but it fed her like, and kept her up, till all at once the collapse came, and now she goes like a ghost. Miss Bethell fussed about her a deal, but there was a sort of enjoying it all in her ways—thank goodness, she is gone now with her visitation and judgments in mercy! she was never pleased until she had made dear Miss Felicy cry, and at last I spoke to Dr. Gooch, who said that would never do—her spirits must be kept up as much as we could—so Miss Rosy was huffed, and she went."

I asked Carr if her mistress would know me. Oh yes, she said, her lady would know me—she knew everybody; she was not out of her senses, I must not fancy that. She was "up and down," sometimes excited, and then low, with fits of wandering delirium. "It is very sad, but I think it is almost worse for poor master than for her," continued the excellent creature. "This great dull house feels like a prison, now there's no company, and nobody even let in that comes to call. He is a good man, poor master is, and very fond of her. So was the other fond of her, and she'd given him her whole heart. They have much to answer for that sundered them—such love as dear Miss Felicy's is not mocked at. She will get better, Dr. Gooch says, but it may be a long while first, and nobody need expect her to be ever again the buoyant lady she was—she'll have to do without her balls and parties, and to live very quiet and retired. Her so given to gaiety, poor dear!"

Next morning the bells were ringing for church, and the sweet peace of a country Sunday reigned over all when Janet came to bring me into her mistress's presence. George, as I left him, gave me a warning to be cheerful, and to avoid exciting topics, and then with a beating heart, and strongly suppressed emotion, I followed the maid through a labyrinth of passages until we came to the silently revolving green baize doors which separated Felicia's apartments from the rest of the house. I heard her voice before I saw her, for a large folding screen concealed the entrance to the outer room, and she was at the moment inquiring of Carr whether I was coming to her, or going to church for morning prayers. I motioned to Janet to go forward, and give me time to collect myself; and passing round the screen, she announced my approach.

"Mrs. Gower is coming, Miss Felicy, and she has rested well after her journey."

"That is good news—if I took a journey, I wonder whether I should rest?" said the plaintive voice of Felicia.

Janet looked from behind the screen, and signed to me to advance. Felicia's back was towards me for a minute—her tall figure draped in a loose white wrapper, her profusion of hair cut and confined in a net, her thin hands and bare arms stretched above her head as the weary stretch them in a spasm of insupportable *ennui.* Carr rose, and dropt a curtsey, and immediately Felicia turned round. She moved to meet me. Oh! her pathetic face! Her countenance was full of tears; my eyes were blinded as I looked at her. She was just in the same way as during the early days of her first grief—or rather, perhaps, as she was during the weeks following her father's journey to Italy.

Know me?—she knew me as well as ever she had done in her life! Whatever Dr. Gooch might previse or apprehend for the future, my darling was as sensible and self-conscious as I was, when I came in thus upon her. She coloured, and her hands trembled as she laid them on my shoulders, and stooped to kiss me; and I thought there was a feeling of shame in her mind as if she feared to be accused of behaving childishly. She apologized for not being downstairs to welcome me on my arrival, but asked nothing of how or why I had come. She seemed to feel it natural that I should be there, made me sit down beside her, and bade the servants leave us to ourselves.

"You will be astonished to find me in such dismantled quarters," she said, glancing shyly about the large bare room. "My own rooms are so hot in this weather that I was glad to move into these, when Dr. Gooch suggested it. The north is a pleasant light, but the view on the other side is prettier. If I could only sleep I should do well—but I sleep no more than I did before I made the change. I begin to feel very ill, and to fear that if I cannot get some rest I shall lose my senses. And that would be so dreadful."

"So dreadful that we will not imagine the possibility of it," said I, faintly smiling.

"I am weak and irritable for want of sleep, and sometimes I cannot keep any hold on my thoughts," she went on. "Do you understand what I mean? You know the broken colours of the kaleidoscope—that is like my mind. Fancies and even phrases go running over it like a nonsense-chase."

"If you can analyze it, you can control it?" I suggested.

"Yes, I can control it to a certain extent—if I could not, I suppose I should be really mad. I wish those bells would cease ringing; but they say when the church-bells ring the devil gets out of hearing."

"An old woman's tale," said I, not well knowing what to say, for already Felicia's pale hollow cheek began to flush.

"There's a deal of truth in fables," rejoined she. "What is the moral of my amulet? *Love cannot die*. Ah! Clare, if I had believed it, I should not be in chains now. You cried on my wedding-day—I cried too, but no one saw me."

"Tears don't much avail. I prayed for you more than I cried. It is church time—shall I read you part of the prayers?" I proposed, for I thought reading might soothe her, while conversation evidently raised her excitement.

She answered me with touching mournfulness: "I have no objection if you think there is any profit in it. God has never given me what I asked for, and it is not much I have asked for lately. It is terrible to feel my duty becoming every day more irksome, and it is not lightened for all my prayers. I am very unhappy—I cannot go on living thus—I shall lose my wits! Then they might shut me up, and use me roughly, which I have never been used to. I don't think George would—the sight of him, his very goodness and forbearance increase my misery. It was wicked to marry him, for I had no true love in my heart—and he has a right to complain."

"But he does not complain; you will never wear out his tender patience. Say what he is to do, and he will do it.—Do you wish him to go away, and leave you, if the sight of him be painful?"

"No—where should he go? If one must go, let it be myself."

"There is no *must* in the case unless you make one. George will not consent to your leaving his house and protection. You are his wife—you have not forfeited any right that gives you. Consider, my darling, that you cannot change what is. You are in an exaggerated mood just now, and I am here that you may do nothing rashly."

"You are like a *douche* of common sense, Clare. Sit here, and I will lie down, and tell you all about it—I have had no one to whom I could open my mind for so long, so very long."

Whether to refuse her confidences, or whether to let her pour out her heart-fulness? Carr had come back again, and stood a little way off, regardful of her mistress. I looked at her face for a clue to discretion. She caught my eye, and as she retired without speaking, I was easier in listening to Felicia's involved and tedious story—a story, all the facts of which I knew. She rambled incoherently, and lost her thread more than once, but it was with intense fervour that she entreated me to say whether I believed that Captain Gresham, during these latter days, had been only playing with her, as Rosy had said.

"It was no fault of mine that we met—as often as we did.—Could he be mocking me? It is a cruel thought! and he seemed so sorry for us both! George was most generous—I would rather have died than injure him! It was all pain together. I suffered Paul too long. I said, at last, that he must go, and never see me more. When we took our farewells, on our knees, Clare, on our knees, for I made him kiss the cross that I had kissed—could he be mocking me *then?* Ah! no—it is a lie, like all the other lies they invented to divide us!—But we were delivered from temptation, and saved from remorse—I forgot everything for a little while, and they brought me down here. Now that I remember again, I wish, I wish I could get out of the world where all would be new, and nothing to remind me of this dreadful misery! I am so afraid in the night-time, that I clutch hold of the thought of God, as the only thought that can save me from falling absolutely under possession of the devil—that old madness of the Scriptures——"

"You cannot do better, and it *will* save you, my darling!" cried I.

"You have faith that it will. Often when I am pleading that I trust in the Lord, something puts it into my heart that I am a hypocrite, only pretending, and that He does not answer me, because He knows I am trying to cheat with false prayers. I wonder whether that old clergyman at Ashencliffe knows anything of the trials of this life, or whether his sermons are all about the other, like fairy-tales?"

The church-doors must have been open, for we could hear the organ and the singing where we sat. We were silent until the music ceased, and then Felicia reverted to my proposal for prayers. I could only nod my acquiescence—all at once the sorrow of the scene had overcome me, and I could not have steadied my voice to read.

Felicia smiled at my emotion, then kissed me affectionately, and said she would say *her* prayer, the only one she remembered that suited her condition; and standing up before the window she recited in a low tone of most passionate pleading that psalm of sorrows:—

"*Out of the depths have I cried unto thee, O Lord: Lord hear my voice: O, let thine ears consider well the voice of my supplications. If thou, Lord, wilt be extreme to mark what is done amiss:*

O Lord, who may abide it? But there is forgiveness with thee, that thou mayst be feared. I look for the Lord: my soul doth wait for him: in his word do I hope. My soul waiteth for the Lord more than they that watch for the morning! I say more than they that watch for the morning. O, my soul, trust in the Lord, for in the Lord there is mercy: and with him is plenteous redemption. And he shall redeem thee from all thy sins."

Long before Felicia came to an end, I had broken down and was sobbing aloud. But she was perfectly abstracted, and wore a countenance of great exaltation. Carr, who had returned at the sound of her mistress's voice, intimated that I had better escape before she observed me, and I made haste to go, lest my poor darling should see my tears, and be brought down from her blissful ecstasy.

"She has a happy memory," said George, talking to me of his wife that evening. "She has by heart psalms and hymns without end. It is a comfort for those poor servants who are never away from her, that this is so. She makes rather free, Janet says, with the name of the devil, but when we were children science had not found him out; he was no myth, but a very energetic and indefatigable personage, and poor Felicia evidently retains her early faith, and does not suppose him to be either dead or in his dotage. When she is delirious, control of speech is lost, but nothing ever escapes her lips that is painful to those who are with her!"

My hapless darling! hers was, indeed, a beautiful soul. It was an inexpressible treasure to those who loved her, that through all her affliction she was never degraded or utterly cast down! She had temporary delusions, but none of them were painful. Each time I went to her she apologized for receiving me in that "destitute chamber," as she called it, but said that her friends never visited her now save one or two, and it gave Janet less trouble to keep in order than her beautiful rooms—Janet and Carr were all the servants she had left, but they were very kind, and she hoped she was grateful. She spoke of her father and others who had helped her to her sorrow, without any resentment or blame—all her blame was for herself. Occasionally she coupled plain terms of uncomplimentary description with names that she mentioned; but she probably uttered only what she had always thought, but had once had control enough to keep to herself. If we all spoke our literal minds concerning our neighbours what a bedlam would the world be!

There was no piano in her room, but her nurses said she did not miss it, for she never wanted to sing—the nearest approach she ever made to singing was in the hush of the twilight, when she would rock herself and murmur a sort of lullaby or cradle song without words. In her fits of garrulous excitement, she seemed to forget all but the whim of the hour: in these low evening moods, she was visibly conscious of her vast calamity. I remember her well on one occasion, see-sawing in a low American chair, and interrupting her sweet, inarticulate song, now and then, to say something. I was in the window-seat with my back to the sunset, and the glow fell on her face—pallid;

tintless as parchment, dry-lipped, her brows depressed above her gloomy sad eyes, her hair ruffled off her forehead, and faded from its bright gold to ashen grey underneath.

"The beautiful Miss Barrington!" Ah! if they could have seen her who had brought her to that pass!

"There is a bow in the clouds every night here—it used only to come with the sunshine in rain at home—how is it, Clare?" was an inquiry she made while gazing at the sumptuous west.

"You see more than I see. I see only level lakes of pale sulphur and purple banks of land, like an upper world in the sky," was my answer, looking behind me.

"It is absurd to suppose that earth, air, and water, are alike to all of us," she rejoined. "You are convinced of God, because you are happy. Since I am so full of sorrows He has set me a bow in the clouds, lest I should quite despair. Rosy said it was all my fancy and conceit—God would never do such a silly thing—Rosy, you must know, is one of the privy counsellors of heaven." She stopt, laughing softly to herself at this notion of Rosy endued with divine wisdom.

Presently she resumed: "The deep waters have gone over my soul! but I was rescued in my own despite—Clare, if I had fallen before my great temptation, what sin! what remorse! It is better thus with me, though bad is the best! What is the mystery of my pain? If our Father pleased, we might all be happy, and instead, he lets us go mad for a season. I will not believe that he made any of us to be lost eternally—or that we were suffered to fall into misery, that he might be glorified in our salvation. Rosy makes the Bible a book of riddles—she perplexes me."

"Never mind words, dear; think only of what you said just now—that you were in a great straight; and you were saved—who but God saved you? As I read, our Father desires the return of all his children."

Felicia fell silent for a time, then fell into her low half-song, I sitting by and the night drawing on. By-and-by, she muttered: "It is not necessary to be a philosopher to know that one's heart is broken. It seems to me that the air is full of fog, but the bow is a perfect arch, and grows brighter as the dark spreads below. Shylock had a ring that Leah gave him when he was a bachelor. Clare, what have you done with my amulet?"

"It is safe in my davenport-drawer, where we locked it up," said I.

"If I had it here, I would wear it for a charm against evil spirits. When Lucy died there was a ribbon round her neck, and a locket with hair under the glass—she asked to be buried with it. I should wish to be buried with Paul's amulet."

In this way, at intervals, she went on talking, until it was so dusk that the trees were colourless, dark masses against a dark sky. Then Carr appeared, and said that rest and be still for all sakes her dear mistress must, to which Felicia urged that she was not tired, and she did not want me to leave her. I promised to stay by her till she slept.

"Till I sleep! ah! if I *could* sleep," said she, but was quite submissive while Janet prepared her for rest.

When she was laid down she begged me not to go—she had so much to say to me.

"Well, Miss Felicy, talk then," said Carr. "I've known you talk yourself to sleep many a time before now, and if you do it to-night, so much the better. I am no friend to sleeping draughts, if natural sleep is by any means to be had, but if you don't nap off before eleven o'clock, you will have this bottle of stuff to drink" (exhibiting a small phial), "and it is not nice I can tell you." The nurse nodded her head decisively, just as she might have done at Felicia naughty a dozen years ago, and my poor darling smiled quite like herself at the odd effect on me of this ancient discipline. I smiled too, and promised to try and be as good as a sleeping-draught.

She had professed to have much to say, but she lay silent for a long while with her hands under her cheek, and her eyes fixed on the shaded lamp in the further room. Presently she began talking to herself, and so, I understood, she would go on sometimes all night. Neither her thoughts nor subjects were continuous, but I always caught her meaning. "Good-night, dear! When will it ever be good-night with me again until the last sleep of all? Enter the beautiful Miss Barrington, with a flourish of trumpets, exit the same to a muffled peal!" Here came a pause, then: "One, two, three, four, how many days since I have seen George? If I were dead, he would not break his heart, because he knows it would be as if we had both escaped out of prison—and yet he loves me more than they all. None of the others would miss me—not papa—not Paul—I am nothing but a sorrowful remembrance to Paul. I have thrown a cloud upon his life—and the sooner cloud and I vanish the happier for him. As for grannie, she is on the way to forget—old age cares most for itself. Clare has her husband and children, and will feel no want when I am gone—but she will be sorry, poor little brown mouse! yes, *very*. Janet will marry the Scotch gardener, and Carr will be left alone—she will weep like a fountain, and be consoled in talking of me. I think I hear the muffled peal already, or is it the wind rising? Strange to hear one's own funeral bells."—Here she relapsed into silence, and was silent for so long that I hoped slumber had fallen upon her perturbed brain; but no, when I bent to look at her, her eyes were wide open, and still fixed on the distant light.

Carr came creeping in with her phial and a glass to receive its contents. Felicia roused from her reverie, and said: "It is of no use, Clare—we go through the same ceremony every night, but kind Nature's sweet restorer never comes. I am not one of God's beloved, for he gives me no sleep. I wish the day were at hand when you might all look at me, and say: "Poor soul, she is at rest. She will never wake any more."

This day was more distant than my darling thought and hoped; she was to have yet an interval of peace; but her present trial was long. She remained at Wych-Elm a few weeks more without any visible improvement, and then went to Ashencliffe at her own desire. Here she stayed till the beginning of winter, and then returned home. Arthur had recalled me before her removal to the sea, and I carried back to Gladestone the most favourable report of her that I could. Dr. Gooch's dictum was that, though sadly overstrained, her mind had not lost its balance, and would not do so unless her malady took a turn that he did not anticipate. But for all that I could say, the old belief prevailed that she was mad.

CHAPTER XIV.

THE FALL OF THE GREAT BETHELL OAKS.

My first visitor after my return to Stoneleigh was Captain Gresham. I never saw a man more broken by misery, and yet I do not know that he was to blame. He took blame to himself, however, and cursed the caution and credulity that had kept him apart from Felicia while there was yet time to repair their mischief:—of the passion that had imperilled both since, he said no word. He could not figure to his imagination his lost love as she was now. He dwelt on the remembrance of her in the early days of their fondness, when he was her Prince Charming, and she his sweet lady of innocence, beauty and truth. Be sure I told him nothing to destroy that fair and tender image. It was not by *their* fault that their fate was so unfortunate.

The dowager sent for me when she heard that I had come back from Wych-Elm. I found her laid up in her room, and Miss Lassells established there with books and work, as if their life were limited now to that narrow space. And so it was.

"I used to think that I should have Felicia, at least, to close my eyes," was the poor old grandmamma's first sentence, and she could not finish it for tears.

Miss Lassells soothed her, and when she was able to listen, I gave such an account of Felicia as I could to console her, without violating the truth. She accepted what I said implicitly.

"God take her to himself, and soon, poor thing!" was her comment on it. "I wish it might please Him to take her before me; then I should go with a free mind, knowing her safe. It is a very cruel position both for her and for George, and one can never be sure what might happen, if George tired of the dreadful restraint." I had confidence in George that he would not tire; that he would guard Felicia in her helplessness as no other friend could, and not claim any praise for the performance of his duty—for he had spoken of it to me as his *duty*.

The poor dowager went on with feeble, fretful indignation: "Her father was always selfish, but Lucilla would not see it.—Here is another proof; he makes Felicia's sad calamity the excuse for staying abroad, and not keeping his promise to her of living half the year at Stoneleigh—that is the substance of his last letter."

I had heard as much from Arthur already, and without surprise. They must have been very sanguine indeed, who expected Mr. Barrington to do anything that did not chime in exactly with his good-will and pleasure!

Perhaps the most grievous face of all that I saw was Squire Sylvester's. He was terribly disappointed for his son. He did not say much, for what can be said in such circumstances? but his sympathy in George's trouble added ten years to his age.

The world does not stand still because one or another of its favourites falls out of the race, and in a shorter time than I care to recollect, people ceased to mention Felicia. She was present to my mind often—*often*. At church where her place was vacant, on the Langhill where she loved to walk, in the cottages where the poor so much missed her bountiful hand; but I learnt by-and-by not to speak of her, as one does learn not to speak of a topic that others avoid, and are visibly weary of. The Manor remained shut up, with only the gardener and his wife for care-takers; and the helpers being all discharged, the gardens ran into wilderness in a summer, as neglected gardens will. Judd domineered over all, a complete lord of misrule. Mr. Barrington never showed himself at Stoneleigh for the space of two years; but the rents and royalties were gathered very closely, and all the good old customs at Christmas were given up. Judd's policy was to squeeze as much out of the property as he could, and to put in as little as possible; and we were given to understand that this was the sum and substance of Mr. Barrington's instructions for its management.

There was a selfish cynicism in this greedy tyranny. "After me the deluge; after Felicia her Uncle Tom"—and why should anything be spared for her Uncle Tom? That was Mr. Barrington's reasoning; and that was how the Great Bethell Oaks, so often threatened, came down at last.

Lady Augusta's extravagance and love of pleasure kept pace with her husband's, and how much money soever they had, they always were in want of a little more. Even Judd grumbled occasionally at the pressure put upon him, but he generally ended by finding something to supply the immediate demand; and there was a gradual disappearance of the fine timber, that had survived former raids, which would have turned poor Mr. Tom Bethell's hair grey had it not gone through that process already. It added a livelier poignancy to his vexation to remember that he had put this compliant Judd in his office; and now the man jeered and defied him, if he tried to speak in defence of the estate. "It was no business of his to meddle with the property—

let him wait till he got it, and then he might manage it to please himself. Till then it was enough for him (Judd) if he managed to please his master, without being plagued by interlopers."

One memorable morning while I sat in the parlour teaching the children their lessons, I observed lame Simeon resting for an unconscionably long time on his broom, and stargazing apparently, as his wont was, between short spells of work. At last I looked out to see if perchance he had fallen asleep in that attitude, but was diverted from every other thought by the view of several men on the Langhill, evidently very busy, and of Mr. Tom Bethell and Judd amongst them, violently gesticulating, as if a quarrel *à outrance* were in loud progress. And that was, in fact, the case. Only that morning, and by the merest chance, had the heir-presumptive learnt that the crowning glory of his inheritance was sold and doomed, and here he was come over, post-haste, in the forlorn hope of rescuing it.

While he railed, and vainly menaced the destroyers with the terrors of the law, strong arms, wielding broad axes, went hard at their task. Many a big limb was lopped that day, and toppled down on the green sward to which it had been a generous shade for ages, and many a noble crest bowed and fell before the universal stroke. For how long the giant boles stood like skeletons upon the hill, stripped of their bark, naked, unsightly, beaten by wind and rain, scorched and bleached by pitiless sun, a ghastly parody of all the trouble that had come upon that house, I cannot tell. But I remember that I was thankful when these mementoes of death and decay vanished, and the green ridge showed only the vast royal roots of them level with the ground.

"We have lived to see strange sights," quoth lame old Simeon. "It is about time we ould folk got us to bed!"

It was of no use for Mr. Barrington to write here, and to write there, protesting that Judd had been too zealous in his service; that he had never meant the destruction of the Bethell Oaks, and that he mourned them sincerely—(no doubt he did—they were not there to cut down, and sell again). The deed was done, and the money in his pocket, and as my little Jack sang with undesigned sentiment:

> Not all the king's horses, nor all the king's men,
> Could set the Great Oaks on the Langhill again!

When this event befel (a vast event in the annals of Stoneleigh) Felicia was partially restored, but not so far restored as to bear telling of it. It was consummated before it was heard of at Wych-Elm, or George had the power of putting a veto upon it in the name of his wife. Being *done*, however, he said nothing; and the facts came to her knowledge first through Rosy Bethell. Felicia had then begun to write to me again, short letters, but quite in her former manner. Here is a brief extract from one referring to the business.

"So the Great Bethell Oaks are down at last! Ichabod! Ichabod! The glory is, indeed, departed! I shall never care to see the dear old home again, so you must come and see me."

CHAPTER XV.

WEARING AWAY.

THERE is a profound pathos in that prayer of troubled Job, to be let alone that he might take comfort a little before going to the land whence he should not return, the land of darkness and the shadow of death.

The death of Felicia has always carried this consolation with it to my mind—that before she left us, she had a few years of rest and quiet peace, when she ceased both to regret and to desire. She never came into Gladeshire any more, but twice after her restoration to health Arthur and I visited Wych-Elm. The first occasion was within a few months of the destruction of the Great Bethell Oaks, and we were the earliest visitors she was permitted to receive.

The year was in its decline, October was far advanced, but the season was fine, and summer airs lingered to the very verge of winter. The interval of his wife's seclusion had not been wasted by George. He had rarely been absent from his home for longer than a day; he had manfully set himself work to do, and had done it. His cottages were re-built, the park was wonderfully beautified by judicious clearings and prunings, the lake was cleansed from weeds, and shone like rippled glass. The old house itself had been all repointed, reglazed, freshened, I know not how, and while a very sad house, had contrived to put on a most home-like, pleasant face. It had impressed me as hot, dreary, airless, when I was there before; now it seemed cheerful and bright as any home that I was ever in. And late as it was in the year, there were flowers in a profusion and variety that Stoneleigh itself could not have more than rivalled.

And George and Felicia themselves? They were happy and contented—absolutely necessary to each other, and perfectly devoted. A vast amount of needless compassion had been wasted upon George while he had been actively busy, living most of his time in the open air, maintaining his natural condition of robust health, and when Felicia gave hopeful signs of recovery, developing spirits to match. Felicia was fair and delicate, more like her mother, as I remember her in her latter days, than like her former self.

We did not see her on the evening of our arrival; but the next morning, a most glorious morning for sunshine, looking from my window before I was dressed, there was she, pacing on the broad eastern terrace, arm-in-arm with George. It was her custom now to retire early, and rise betimes. The clear, brisk sweetness of the morning gave her strength for the day; and when we met in the breakfast-parlour, her cheeks had a soft rose, and her beautiful eyes shone with the brightness of the tonic air. We looked at each other long and wistfully, but had not much to say until we were alone; and even then Felicia was more meditative and silently retrospective than conversational. She had her needlework, pretty toy-work, her water-colour drawing, and music to fill her time, and seemed never less alone than when alone. She was very much changed, very placid, tranquil—apathetic almost.

For a week we were together, some days for hours at a time, but to certain circumstances she never made any reference—to her illness, for instance, and to the events that preceded it. She liked to speak of George chiefly, and she manifested a degree of curiosity about old friends and neighbours, especially old friends and neighbours amongst the poor; but the lively, intelligent interest she had once taken in a thousand things and people was quite extinguished. Her life had fallen altogether into a lower key. Her tone was that of a person who has done with changes, who just sits still, and lets the world run by with the easy philosophy of elderhood. She had not, I think, a care beyond the present moment. George was exquisitely good to her. I never witnessed a more tender solicitude than his, repaid by a more affectionate gratitude than hers.

"Dear old George, what a blessing you are to

me!" she would exclaim with the kindliest face, when he brought her flowers or something else in the middle of the morning, to be sure that she was not tiring herself with overmuch talk.

He need not have been afraid. If she had her work, I had mine too, and we were more silent often than given to chat. Felicia would ask a question. If I answered it briefly, she listened; if I enlarged at all, I soon lost her attention. Yet she liked to keep me with her, for whenever I made a move to slip quietly away, and leave her to herself, she would arrest my flight: "Don't run away, Clare. I like to have you by, if it be only to look at."

Then at intervals she would make some remark, or give me some confidence that set me thinking. Once it was:—

"No one knows but myself how excellent George is. I am sorry for him that we have no children; but he says that he would rather have had me for his wife, poor body as I am, than any other woman in the world. However, I shall be like mamma—I shall die young. I don't feel as if the springs of life in me would last much longer."

She did not add what I know was in her thoughts—that when she was gone, George might marry another wife.

She went on to speak of blind Mary, and told me that George had brought her down to Wych-Elm, and boarded her with the village schoolmistress; and the next day when we went out, she took me to see this strange, perplexing being. It was a kindness to feed and shelter her; for she was utterly incapable of providing for herself, unless by the exercise of her native craft and cunning with which she had so long imposed on the benevolent. She was not a poor pensioner to rejoice the heart of a benefactor, but George had decided that it was his duty to rescue her from misery, and he did, in fact, maintain her until she died.

Of her father and Lady Augusta, Felicia conversed freely. To their vast pride and satisfaction they had a son (Felicia had not seen her little brother), and they were trying, not very effectually, to be more prudent in their expenditure, with a view to the bringing-up and putting-out in life of this precious boy. Mr. Barrington had been at Wych-Elm occasionally for half a day at a time since his daughter began to recover, and they were all friends together. Yet as she talked of them there was a strain of feeling as if she knew herself outside of the world they lived in—a world where there were still hopes, prospects, expectations, and the uncertainties of a future—all things she had done with. After a while this current of thought in her saddened me, and I tried to raise her imagination; but she only laughed at me, and said: "Dear little Clare, as sanguine as ever! Always anticipating a new and better lease of life!"

That is my way—why should we borrow trouble? why should we die before our day comes? However, after that rallying check from my darling, I said no more; in fact, I believe she knew and foreknew for herself all that was to be far better than any of us.

There is not much to tell of this visit when

I come to recall it. Every day was alike. The calm monotonous routine and atmosphere of the place had its influence on me; and when Arthur took me away at the end of it, I went contentedly, and felt glad that I had seen and left Felicia in such good case.

Our second visit to Wych-Elm was in the following year, but earlier in the season, and Mab Bethell travelled with us for the advantage of an escort. Mab was Felicia's favourite amongst her cousins. Bobby, her special boy, also came from Eton while we were there, and partridge-shooting being in progress, there was more stir and vivacity about the old house than during our former stay. But Felicia's mode of life was much the same. She was no stronger, but rather the reverse. It was not an absolute rule for her to entertain her guests; it appeared to me that her love of solitude increased, but that for George's sake, she did her utmost to be sociable. Mab was a great help, a dear, good, beautiful girl, very happy-tempered and unselfish. Felicia had a growing fondness for her, and from this time she was almost as much at Wych-Elm as at Ringwood while Felicia lived. She could be very well spared at home, where there were so many girls grown up, and none yet married. It struck me that Felicia had a design in her friendship for Mab, but Mab was quite unconscious of it, for her affections were already fixed; and the event did not realize Felicia's secret wish, as I interpreted it. However, before her change came, she knew the truth.

Three years, or nearly three years, elapsed between this, our second visit, to Wych-Elm, and my last. The last was long talked of, and more than once or twice deferred for home reasons. Finally we set off one day to London, where Arthur had business to transact, connected with the will of a deceased relative; and I wrote a line on the evening of our arrival telling Felicia, whom I knew to be at Wych-Elm, that I would run down on the morrow by the noon train, and spend a few hours with her while he was engaged with the lawyers. I expected no answer, and, indeed, there was no time for any, unless by telegraph; yet I was surprised not to find some servant or carriage to meet me when I reached the station for Wych-Elm. Still as it was fine weather, and the distance nothing to me, I should have set off to walk across the fields, had not the station-master recognized me as a former visitor at the great house, and explained to me what trouble was there.

"Mrs. Sylvester-Constable is very ill, ma'am," he said. "One of the London doctors arrived by the last train."

"Ill!" I cried. "Indeed, I had not heard a word of it. She was well at the beginning of the week!"

"It has been very quick—fever, caught as they think, in the village. There was no hope this morning."

While the station-master was still speaking, one of the Wych-Elm carriages drove up, and out sprang Dr. Gooch. He knew me, though I had seen him but once, and that before Felicia's marriage. His natural thought was that I was hastening to my friend in her extremity, and taking my hand kindly, he said:—

"You are too late, Mrs. Gower, too late! That dear lady is with her best friend now; and you must let me escort you back to town."

I was anxious to go forward, but the physician firmly advised my return to my husband, assuring me that the time to be of use was past, and the time to be of comfort to the bereaved husband not come; and that the fever being highly dangerous, I should do wrong to place myself in contact with it to no purpose. I allowed him to over-rule me, and Arthur agreed that it was right, but somehow, I have regretted it since. So sudden—without warning, and all over! I could not realize the event as true until we were settled at home again, and week after week went by without bringing me any more letters from Felicia.

She was buried at Wych-Elm. The dowager wished her to be laid with her own family in the vault at Stoneleigh, but George said No; where she was buried, he would be buried, and his last home must be with the old Constables, whose successor he was. Mr. Barrington was at Florence when his daughter died, and he did not come home. He could not have arrived in time for her funeral, and there was nothing to come for after. He and Lady Augusta had settled permanently at Florence, and the intercourse between the father and daughter had been so long and constantly interrupted, that except for what he lost of income by her death, it is probable that he never missed her.

Felicia had requested her husband to send to me all her letters, papers, journals to be looked over and destroyed. With them arrived a strong box containing, amongst other things, mementoes to her friends. It was a most melancholy task that I had. She must have spent many a day arranging her sad bequest, which formed a complete history of her life. If she had not often spoken of it in recent years, she had not thought the less. Amongst the gifts the name of her Cousin Rosy was attached to the turquoise bracelet that she had coveted to wear at a certain ball I remembered long ago, and her lovely set of opals and diamonds was a treasure bequeathed to her Cousin Mab. Mab was then on the eve of her marriage with Captain Gresham. Round the case containing the jewels was folded the red ribbon and cross which has been spoken of. I gave them into Captain Gresham's own hand to carry to Mab; he recognized the ribbon and its ornament, yellow with lying by, and said that he should take *that* for his keepsake.

This courtship had been slow and uneasy. Conscience, or old affection, plagued Felicia's lover for many a year after he lost her. Yet there were intervals in his regret when Mab Bethell's beauty and sweetness had a salutary charm. He liked Mrs. Bethell. Mab resembled her most of her girls, and Fairfield and Ringwood were neighbours. He resisted consolation for a long while, resented it almost, but at each meeting he grew more into tender friendship with Mab, who adored him; and at last, to the satisfaction of their friends on both sides, they became engaged.

Mab told the news to Felicia herself (all the old story was familiar to her), and Felicia kissed and blessed her with a promise that she would be a happy woman. "Paul was not perfect, but his imperfections are of a sort to endear him to his wife. You know *we* were to have been married once, but it was broken off, and I married George instead —I am glad he has chosen you, Mab; for you are my darling."

Felicia's death delayed the marriage for a few months, and the Bethells stayed at Ringwood until it was over. Then they came to rule and reign at Stoneleigh. The new squire found everything in the utmost disorder, from neglect, waste, and peculation; and though he has been long enough master now to have reduced things into tolerable condition, he still grumbles and looks more careworn, haggard, and discontented than ever. He declares that he is poorer, too, for all the property is deeply encumbered, and the name of being rich has set his sons on being extravagant. If he inherited a gold mine, it is my belief that he would still not have enough; for covetousness and discontent are the habit of his mind.

EPILOGUE.

Arthur and I were in London during that recent exhibition of pictures when the portrait of Felicia attracted so much attention. One afternoon he had left me, and I was resting in front of it, waiting for his return, and thinking my own thoughts, when there sauntered into the room a group of people all belonging to this history. First came Mr. Barrington, with a handsome little boy by the hand, in a velvet suit—a brown-faced impetuous little boy, a complete tyrant to his father, at whose arm, as he halted before the portrait of Felicia, he tugged right manfully.

"See, Frank, look at this pretty fairy girl

—she was your sister," said the old gentleman—Mr. Barrington was quite the old gentleman now, but always with his gay and popular air.

The child was instantly still, and gazed up solemnly at the lovely picture, and then called out: "Mamma, this is sissy, who is in heaven." I thought it pretty that they had taught him so to think of her.

Lady Augusta advanced. She looked younger since her marriage, and more gracious and pleasant. She took the boy's other hand: "Poor Felicia!" I heard her mumur, and they all loitered on together in silence, but quite free from any emotion. They did not observe me, and I let them pass unchallenged.

Some ten minutes later appeared George Sylvester, evidently by the manner of him, come to find out the picture. When it caught his eye, he came quickly that way, and I was glad that he had it for a minute to himself. He was looking hale, hearty, and good as ever, but his countenance saddened as he gazed. Then pushed in a sudden throng of strangers, and he turned to seek a seat where I still rested. He recognized me, and instantly cheered up.

"Ah! Mrs. Gower, what a pleasure to see you!" cried he. "You, too, have come to look at our darling. The treasure is mine now. I have bought it from Mr. Bethell. Felicia will not return to Stoneleigh any more—she will go down to keep me company in my solitude at Wych-Elm."

George Sylvester had mourned his wife with a long fidelity; he had given her no successor in his heart or his home. It was only the other day that his old father, the Squire of Bylands, who lives still, told me that his son had been prevailed on at last to choose him another wife, and that his choice had fallen upon a lady whom all his friends approved.

The beautiful Miss Barrington never reappeared in the gay world she once adorned after her second mysterious illness and seclusion. Some who knew her well in the brief season of her triumph, have inquired, since her death, what had become of her—that I suppose is the way of the world. It talks for nine days over a tragedy, and then the actors in it are forgotten by all save the few who love them.

FINIS.

LONDON
PRINTED BY SMITH, ELDER AND CO.,
OLD BAILEY, E.C.

CPSIA information can be obtained
at www.ICGtesting.com
Printed in the USA
LVHW040839070223
738797LV00003B/251